Silent Lee
and the
Adventure
of the
Side Door
Key

Silent Lee

and the
Adventure
of the
Side Door
Key

ALEX
HIAM

Silent Lee

Webster Press, LLC

Published by
Webster Press, LLC

ISBN: 978-1-63558-011-2
eISBN: 978-1-63558-012-9

Cover and Interior Design: GKS Creative
Copyediting: Kim Bookless
Proofreading: Melanie Zimmerman
Project Management: The Cadence Group

This is a work of fiction. Names, characters, places and incidents either are the product of the author's imagination or are used fictitiously. Any resemblance to actual persons, living or dead, events, or locales is entirely coincidental.

This book is inspired by all my children and their
love of good stories. I dedicate the book to them,
and most notably to my daughter Sadie,
who edited the first draft when she was about
the same age as Silent Lee.
Thanks!

Her heart racing, she scrambled up the attic stairs and paused at the top, peering into the dim space with its rough old dark wood rafters sweeping down to meet the floor on either side.

The birdcage was sitting in the middle of the room beside her sleeping bag. A rectangle of sunlight filtered in through the attic window and illuminated the cage brightly. In the cage was a lushly leafed branch that had not been there before, and on the branch was perched an amazing blue finch.

The finch turned, bright-eyed, to study her. She tiptoed over, not wanting to scare it away, but it seemed unafraid. It hopped to the end of the branch and stuck its bill through a gap in the wire. It was holding a thin strip of paper. The paper seemed to have something written on it, and the handwriting was strangely familiar.

About Magic:

Stories often employ magic, but real people seldom do. That has lead to a lot of unfortunate misconceptions about what magic is and how to do it. Here are a few facts, just to help set the record straight.

First, a ward is a spell that blocks other spells. If you're not the only one who can use magic, then you better start by perfecting your wards. It's good to be able to avoid spells aimed at you by unscrupulous magic-workers. Unfortunately, magic, like anything powerful, is prone to misuse.

A weaving is a spell that pulls in natural, everyday sources of power, like the wind (if you want to lift something) or emotions (if you want to help someone feel more confident). Many of the major spells are woven out of forces of nature. It takes years to learn to weave a beautiful tapestry from thread, and so it is with magical weavings. Silent and her classmates at The Girl's Academy of Latin and Alchemy (GALA) study the magical arts for many years. Fortunately, Silent is quite a good student and able to do more magic than most. She will need all her skills and talent in the adventure that follows. . .

CHAPTER 1

Returning to Aunt Gen's

The birdcage was in the attic, closed up inside a dusty wooden box. On the box was written in faded handwriting: *My Birdcage. Handle With Respect. For true heirs of Generous Lee only. Silent, this probably means you. Tell your mother to stuff it. She can't have my birdcage even if she wants it, although she probably won't.*

Silent read the label with a frown, puzzled not only by the oddity of the message but also by how old and faded it was. She had been away from Great Aunt Gen's house for only a month. But time was complex when it came to Generous Lee, who had lived mostly in a world that was a full century out of date.

Silent was raised in that world and rarely visited the present-day world her mother inhabited. She loved Aunt Gen's world almost as much as she loved Aunt Gen, and it had been quite a shock to have to leave both behind. (But more about that in a page or two . . .)

Sie (pronounced like pie and, of course, Silent's nickname) popped the latch, hinged the dusty box open, and lifted out the birdcage. Underneath it was an envelope labeled *Birth Certificates* (also in Aunt Gen's loopy old handwriting). She'd recently learned that modern schools expect you to have one, so she slipped the envelope into a pocket on her skirt. (Yes, her skirt had pockets—Aunt Gen believed clothing should, above all, be functional.) Then she turned her attention back to the more interesting find, the birdcage itself.

It was bulky and hard to carry down the attic stairs. Sie was on the small side for fourteen, and her arms were aching by the time she arrived in the long, narrow living room of Aunt Gen's townhouse. "I want this," she said, resting the cage on the floor for a moment.

"*Really*, Silent?" her mother's lips were pursed in disapproval. "I doubt that old thing will even fit in the taxi. Why don't you find a *proper* memento?" She glanced around the room. "There's a pair of silver candlesticks on the mantle. Bound to be valuable. Oh, and give me your house keys. You won't be needing them anymore." She held out her hand.

Silent just stood there.

"Keys!" her mother demanded.

"I don't have any. I want to take the birdcage. Please."

Her mother scowled. "If you must. At least *I* won't have to squeeze in next to it. I'm not going to ride back with you. But I don't see the point. You don't have any birds."

"Uh, no. I guess not." Silent recalled how Aunt Gen's brightly colored finches used to sing so happily in the sun by the big bow windows overlooking Newbury Street. *Where had they gone?* she wondered. *And how did the cage end up in a box in the attic?* Last time she'd been there—been home—the cage was on display in the living room, like usual. She would take it. And remember.

Her mother (whose name was Mauvaise Lee), a tall, unsmiling woman in a long gray raincoat, moved toward the front door. She was carrying her own mementos, a pair of sterling silver teapots. They were the largest pieces from Aunt Gen's silver set and thus the most valuable. The last time she'd visited, she'd taken a silver sugar bowl (Sie figured she'd hidden it in her overcoat pocket; there'd been an odd bulge), and Auntie had retrieved it at considerable expense a few days later from Suffolk Pawnbrokers on Washington Street. But of course Sie would not be able to buy anything back, now that Aunt Generous was gone. *Why would my mother rob us,* she wondered.

Sie knew everything in that house by heart because she had grown up there, always with her cheerful Great Aunt Generous to care for her. Her mother traveled constantly for work, so it had always seemed natural for Sie to live with Aunt Gen.

As her aunt grew too old to run up and down the stairs of the three-story row house, Sie grew big enough to do most of the housekeeping and to bring her aunt a tea tray beside the singing birds each day after school. She would even go out, basket on her arm, to shop at the fruit market, bakery, and butcher's on their block. But *that* was the *other* version of their block. It was in the world Aunt Gen preferred, not the noisy modern world in which her mother lived.

Until a month ago, Silent had attended the Girl's Academy of Latin and Alchemy—"GALA" for short—where the students and teachers seemed very old fashioned. But the classics were what mattered to Aunt Gen: Ancient Latin, Greek, Music, Geometry, English Composition, Alchemy levels one through seven, and electives in Oil Painting, Herbalism, Levitation, Spell-weaving, Warding, Illusions, and so on. She did quite well at the school. However, all that was in the past.

Sie had always found her classes stimulating, but her mother would complain about the school whenever she'd visit. "It sounds horribly out of date," she'd say, or, "What kind of career will she possibly be qualified for? I don't intend to support her, you know!" But Aunt Gen would just smile and say, "Don't you have to be in Cairo for breakfast?" and Sie's mother would rush off to the airport again and be gone for months at a time.

Auntie said her mother was a spy, but her mother said she worked for an international spice distributor. Spies or spices? Sie had no way of knowing for sure.

Her mother actually *brought* them spices, such as gummy lumps of olibanum for Sie's birthday (she had no idea what to do with them). For Christmas, Mother was absent but a tin arrived by mail, wrapped in brown paper. Inside were pungent saffron spears, the tiny stamens of a rare poppy that Aunt Gen said lived in the mountains of Afghanistan. But why was Mother in the mountains of Afghanistan? Another Christmas, the mailman delivered a wooden box with smelly powders labeled Anardana, Amchur, and Ajowan. In the end, all the gifts were shoved to the rear of the pantry and forgotten.

"Deep cover," Aunt Gen would say as she held her nose and examined a gift at arm's length. "Whatever her mission, she must be under deep cover."

Standing there in Auntie's house, thinking about the past, made Silent sad. "I miss Auntie," she said.

"I don't," her mother announced. "Have you got the side door key? It's an old one, antique, on a string. I thought she'd lent it to you."

Silent shrugged. "I don't know. I—I must've left it here when Auntie got sick and you took me to stay with the cousins."

CHAPTER 2

The Cousins

The cousins were a family of five boys: eight-year-old twins, Hard and Tough (the family had a somewhat odd approach to names), and sixteen-year-old triplets, Sandy, Rocky, and Muddy. They were always wrestling with one another. Their parents shouted at them a great deal.

The twins shared the small bedroom, the triplets slept in the next biggest room, and their parents, who occupied the master bedroom, kept their door locked to prevent the boys from destroying it (they tended to break table legs and knock over lamps). There was another guest room, but it was locked, too—ready, the cousins' mother would say, for the day when she would start running a bed and breakfast inn out of their house. And so Sie had been given a sleeping bag, along with a kerosene lantern and box of strike-anywhere matches, and sent to the attic.

The cousins were actually second cousins or maybe third, their mother being a distant relation of Aunt Generous. Silent had never even heard of them until her mother brought her there after . . . (she still didn't like to think of it) . . . her aunt's death.

The worst thing about the situation was not that she had to live in the attic. Aside from missing Auntie terribly, the really awful thing was that Sie could no longer go to her own school. Instead, she was bundled off on a strange yellow bus to a noisy school where no one wore uniforms or knew their Latin declinations and students talked to each other by typing messages into shiny tablets they kept in their pockets.

The school, and the modern century in which it was located, were both new to her. Things seemed noisy and strange and confusing, and her friends from her old school were not there. At *all*. They were not only in a different neighborhood; they were in a different century. No chance of catching up with them on the weekend. (And this was the school that demanded a birth certificate—as if there were any doubt she had been born, since she clearly was alive. But they said they needed it to register her properly and kept putting notes about it in her cubby to take home. Not realizing, of course, that "home" was just an attic and there wasn't any adult there who cared to read notes from school.)

Now her mother had shown up in a taxi straight from the airport and taken her back to Aunt Gen's house for one last visit before it would be sold. But why had her mother bothered? It was not like her to be sentimental. Still, there they were with their mementos, and the taxi was waiting for them outside.

"I *can* take care of myself," Sie said. "If I could just stay here."

"You're going back to Yarmouth Street." (The cousins lived in a run-down brick house sandwiched between two elegant townhouses at 4 1/2 Yarmouth Street.) "I'm paying them to keep you there. I trust you won't be a bother? Well, let's hope not. You're small and you don't make much noise. When did you last see that key?"

"Um, I guess when I last went to GALA," Sie said. Actually, the key was dangling from its string around Sie's neck, but the more her mother asked, the more determined Sie felt about keeping it. She was glad to be wearing an old-fashioned white blouse with a collar and to have tucked in the key when she got dressed that morning. (Her clothing, what she'd packed in her overnight bag when she left Aunt Gen's, was quite old fashioned since it came from the other world.)

"You really don't know where that key is? Hmm." Her mother's gaze was hard. "It better turn up when I go through her things, or we'll have to work on your memory. All right, off you go. The meter's still running on that taxi."

"I didn't see a For Sale sign. Who's buying the house?"

"Don't ask questions." Her mother waved her through the front door (which until a month ago, Sie had barely ever used) and along the sidewalk to the taxi. The driver did not get out to help, and it took Sie a few tries to figure out that she had to lay the birdcage on its side and slide it in. But soon she was squeezed in beside it and her mother was reminding the driver of the cousins' address and slamming Sie's door.

As the taxi pulled away from the curb, there was a loud honking. Another car, a black SUV with tinted windows, cut across traffic to take their space. However, Sie did not give it much thought because she was focused on the house itself, peering over her shoulder at the window boxes overflowing with flowers and the graceful bow windows through which they used to watch the busy sidewalk as they sipped their afternoon tea.

It's teatime, she thought, *but I'll never have tea with Aunt Gen again.* And then she did something she never did. She began to cry.

The taxi driver turned up his radio. It was a baseball game. The announcer sounded excited but she had no idea why. She'd never watched TV until she moved to the cousins' house; nor had she listened to the radio. And whatever those hand-sized shiny things were that you could talk to or play games on or listen to music on . . . they seemed interesting, but she missed the serenity and sweetness of her old life. When you wanted music at Aunt Gen's, you sat down at the harpsichord or pulled out the stringed instruments. Auntie liked to play the small ones—violin or viola, mostly—while Sie preferred the *thrum* of the deep-voiced cello weaving through a Bach melody.

The memory brought more tears. She pushed them away and bit her lip. It would not do to let the cousins see her cry. Anyway, Silent never cried. It was a point of pride to her.

Nor would it do to let the cousins see the birdcage. She imagined they would find a way to break it at once. With that thought in mind, she asked the driver to let her out a few doors down from the rear entrance (which was where they hid a spare house key, making it Sie's regular entrance because they had not given her a key of her own). Approaching cautiously on foot, she listened for signs of shouting and only entered when she realized the house was quiet. The family must have gone somewhere, not bothering to wait for her. Maybe out to lunch. But that was normal. Their minivan did not have enough seats for her to ride along on outings, anyway.

She found the spare key under the pot of dead geraniums and let herself into the kitchen. Flies buzzed over an open pizza box as she maneuvered the birdcage through the mess and up the staircase. Panting, she finally climbed the attic stairs and made it to her "room" under the eaves.

She put the birdcage down with a *thump* on the unfinished wood plank floor and cried a little more. Then she dried her eyes, hung her sweater on one of the nails she had banged into rafters to substitute for a closet, and pulled the old-fashioned key out of her shirt. Fingering it, she thought about the door it opened.

When she was little, she had not wondered about that door, but of course, as she grew older she realized it must be special. Auntie always called it the "side door." It was lower and narrower than most doors and made of very deep brown wood with that subtle glow only found in the oldest of antiques. It had a doorknob of soft old brass. There was a brass keyhole in the side door. And as far as she knew, the key around her neck was the only one in the world—correction, in *either* world—that opened the door.

CHAPTER 3

The Side Door

When you left Auntie's house by the side door, you found yourself stepping down into the side garden with its spring lilacs, summer sunflowers, and autumn chrysanthemums. In winter, there was always a dusting of fresh snow. A narrow path lead to a black iron gate and then out to the sidewalk on Newbury Street. But Newbury Street was not the same when you left by the side door. The rush of motorized vehicles was replaced by the *clop clop* of horse-drawn carriages and only an occasional car—elegant, shiny, and black, with swooping fenders.

Through the side door, there were far fewer stores and restaurants. Most of the houses were actual residences, with mothers taking their babies out for a stroll in big black perambulators or maids hurrying back from the local meat and fruit stands with baskets of dinner ingredients. Sie knew many of the people well enough to smile and say good morning to them on the way to school.

School was a ten-minute walk from Auntie's townhouse at 281 Newbury Street. To get to school, she would head up Newbury, cross Gloucester, Fairfield, and Exeter, take a left on Dartmouth Street, and cross Commonwealth Avenue to where a big red brick building occupied a double corner lot.

The school building had a floral-patterned black iron fence and high ironwork doors that were locked tight when school was not in session. But each morning they were thrown open and the students funneled through a little room entirely covered in bright, tiny ceramic tiles. From there, they stepped up into a grand entry hall where the headmistress, a short, plump, cheerful woman in a brocaded robe, greeted each of them by name and sent them off to their first class of the day.

But the strange thing was, if you went out the front door of Aunt Gen's house, you would find yourself on a very different sidewalk, modern and loud with truck motors and taxicab horns, and you would not recognize anyone hurrying along with their shopping bags or briefcases. And when you got to school, *the* school, Silent's wonderful, favorite place to go, the gates were permanently locked, the window blinds were down, and a general look of neglect and decay told you that no one had used the building for a very long time.

Recently, when passing it by, Sie had noticed that the high iron gates were cracked open and the inner door was ajar, inviting a more closeup peek. The entry hall was still tiled from floor to ceiling, just as it should have been, although looking dusty and unused. But a strange man had come and said, "What do you think you're doing?" and she had stammered that she used to go to school there, and he had looked quite disbelieving and told her to stop trespassing. "It's not a school, it's *never* been a school," he snapped. "The school's across the street."

Sie must have looked quite taken aback. Her school had always been in that building, and the building across the street was just apartments; and yet, in this strange, modern, front-door world, there was for some reason a sign next door for a school she had never heard of. She swung back to the grumpy man. "That's not *my* school. This is."

He frowned. "Look, you can't come in, period. I'm the caretaker, and no one's allowed in except contractors."

"Contractors?"

Sie had looked so genuinely puzzled that he had unbent enough to add, "They're working on it for a Saudi Arabian prince whose daughter plans to move to Boston. The project's going to take seven years. Goodbye."

Sie had struggled to digest this news, and in the end had given up. It was better just to leave by Aunt Gen's side door, and the key allowed her to do that whenever she pleased.

But at the cousins' there was no side door. She was stuck in the modern world—the one where her mother apparently worked as a spy or a spice importer in places so distant that she rarely visited her own daughter.

So why had her mother suddenly shown up and taken such an interest in Auntie's house? Was it true that she had to sell it? Then they wouldn't have a house at all. Her mother didn't seem to have one. As far as Sie could tell, she lived in hotels. And on airplanes, flying from one hotel to another.

Maybe, Sie thought, *if the house sells and Mother gets some money, I could at least ask her to buy me a mattress.* But would a mattress fit up the attic stairs? The birdcage barely fit. Sie had scraped her knuckles on the rough wood trying to get it up there.

She sighed and sat down on her sleeping bag. There were some books stacked next to it, books she had brought in her overstuffed bag when she'd first come there. She'd read all of them at least once by now. Why hadn't she gone into Auntie's library and gotten more books? That would have been the sensible thing. Mother was, she was sorry to admit, right. An empty birdcage was a silly thing to bring with her.

She glanced at the birdcage and wished that it was still full of colorful finches—and that Auntie was still around to enjoy them. And that was when she noticed that she could actually hear birdsong. It was faint and distant, but it definitely sounded like birds, Auntie's birds . . . tropical finches twittering to each other companionably.

She jumped up from the sleeping bag and tiptoed toward the birdcage. A ray of dusty sunlight was coming in from where the sun was about to set over the rooftops. It illuminated the aged copper floor of the cage. The patch of sun was wavy, perhaps from the old wavy glass in the attic window. Actually, it was rippling. Like wavelets in a pond. Sie leaned over to stare through the bars. She would have opened the door to the cage to get a better look, but the cage did not have a door. Caring for the birds was one chore that Sie had never done, and she wasn't clear on how her aunt did it. Now Sie thought she knew why. The bottom of the cage was so ripply and bright that she could see through it. Beneath it, she could faintly make out leafy green trees and flitting birds.

The birds began to rise up through the floor of the cage and fly around and around in it, their songs ringing in that narrow, dark attic space.

A tree pushed one of its branches up into the cage. It had lovely green leaves, bright blue flowers, and little yellow berries, which the finches seemed to like.

And then the cage was back to normal with its solid copper bottom, except now it was full of happy, singing, flapping, twittering finches and a flowering branch. "Oh my," Sie said, staring. "So *that's* where Auntie's birds came from!" Although, in truth, she did not know exactly where they had come from. Only that it was a world full of flowers and trees and brightly colored birds, and that the birdcage could act as a window into it.

Like my side door, Sie thought. *I suppose the birds come and go when they please.* "They probably just liked Auntie," she added, speaking out loud to herself. "And they visited her so much that it seemed as if they lived in the cage." *But,* her thoughts went on, *they were never caged at all. It just looked like they were.* The thought brought a smile to her face. It seemed so very hopeful.

CHAPTER 4

Abandoned

She'd suffered through several weeks of the new school without registering properly, and then school had ended. Her English teacher (she'd excelled in his class) suggested she apply to Boston Latin School for ninth grade. But when she asked how to do that at the school office, she'd been told to get her papers in order first. Apparently she'd need a birth certificate even to sign up for the entry exam, which they told her she'd already missed. There was pressure from Washington D.C. to prove students aren't aliens (if they only knew!) by requiring identification. Things seemed a lot more complicated in the modern world. *Oh well,* she thought as she pulled Aunt Gen's envelope out of her pocket and set it down beside her sleeping bag. *I guess I'll work on that tomorrow. Or the next day. Plenty of time, now that summer vacation's begun.*

And that, Sie finally realized, *must be why the cousins are gone.*

She had first suspected they were gone when they did not come home for dinner. She was *certain* she'd been forgotten when they were still absent in the morning. *But where could they be?* She wondered if anyone, anywhere, would be willing to have the cousins as guests. The result would be quite destructive, she imagined as she surveyed their house. Splintered chairs lay beneath the dining table. A picture, its glass cracked, hung crooked above the fireplace mantle. And broken toy cars, trucks, and airplanes littered the living room floor.

The boys had apparently been building a city in the living room: Lego and wood-block buildings with toy vehicles driving in between. But it seemed like a terrible disaster, maybe several disasters, had befallen the inhabitants. Buildings were tipped over or crumbling, cars overturned, planes crash-landed into trains, and headless plastic figures garishly daubed with sticky red paint lay beneath the rubble. Various superheroes made of bright colored plastic were arrayed around a large dinosaur. One was dangling from its mouth. An alien spaceship swung from a light fixture.

Sie worked her way carefully through the destruction and into the kitchen, where dirty cereal bowls were heaped in the sink and boxes of the boys' favorite cereals were still open, one of them tipped over and spilling on the kitchen counter. *A fast departure after breakfast yesterday,* Sie concluded. *And still gone this morning. Hmm.*

She opened the fridge. The milk carton was almost finished and the shelves were surprisingly empty. There was a forgotten head of iceberg lettuce, black with mildew in its clear plastic wrapper, in the bottom of a crisper drawer. Mustard and ketchup bottles occupied a small shelf on the inside of the door. An extra large bottle of ranch dressing was on its side on a middle shelf in a pool of sticky white goo (the boys rarely screwed on a lid all the way). There was nothing else in the fridge. Nothing at all. *So,* she thought, *they tossed their leftovers and didn't go shopping for more, which suggests a long trip. Without me.*

She closed the fridge and went to a cupboard, where she found a tin of biscuits, old-fashioned buttery ones that only she liked (or else the boys would have eaten them). She helped herself to two, along with a quarter cup of milk (all that was left), and sat down at the kitchen island to think.

Not even a note, she thought, pushing the pizza boxes aside. *How rude!* But her mother had been in town. What might her mother have told the cousins' parents? That she was coming to get her? Most likely, yes. And they might have thought that this meant Silent was being taken away for the summer. A normal mother would have done just that. Not just for the day, first to circle around Boston in a taxi so her mother could visit department stores; then, as the day was almost over and Sie had been left waiting in the taxi a half dozen times, an oh-so-brief visit to Aunt Gen's house . . .

A tear welled up in one eye, but she wiped it sternly away. "Oh well," she told herself, putting down the empty glass. "At least I get to make my own summer plans. But it would help if I had some money."

CHAPTER 5

The Boy Down the Block

Raahi did not like it when his classmates called him a bookworm. Bookworms ate books—they didn't read them. And what was wrong with reading books, anyway? But he knew his classmates would have teased him, no matter whether he read or not. They thought his name was strange, and someone had spread a rumor that he was descended from a raj or king. That, apparently, was enough to ensure he'd be the object of teasing. His very thick glasses and a tendency to bump into people probably didn't help either.

If he'd been a straight A student, perhaps it would have been all right, but his mind was often far away, caught up in some old book he'd scrounged from a recycling bin outside one of the old houses in his neighborhood. He found his assigned readings terribly boring. So he was "neither fish nor fowl," as the old authors used to put it—thick glasses and nearly blind, but not a straight A nerd to go with his nerdish appearance. He was that most outside of all outsiders: an intellectual eccentric. (That he'd aced the test and gotten into the prestigious Boston Latin School for next year didn't change anything—in fact, he'd decided it would only make things worse and hadn't mentioned it.)

He'd thought he was the most peculiar student in the entire school until, near the end of the semester, that girl had shown up in her old-fashioned pleated wool skirts, her old-fashioned black leather lace-up boots, and her gray stockings. Not to mention the antique-looking blouses with what looked like real pearl buttons. She dressed like someone in a black-and-white picture from one of the very old magazines he would occasionally dig out of the underground stacks at the Boston Public Library to entertain himself with glimpses of what Boston used to be.

While she appeared to have stepped straight out of history, it wasn't her appearance that marked her as the ultimate outsider at their school. It was her strangely piercing and thoughtful dark brown eyes, large, rarely blinking, that took in everything and betrayed nothing. And even more, it was what she said on those rare occasions when a teacher would corner her and insist that she speak.

Once, in science class, the teacher had asked her to define sulfur. "Now, please," he had insisted.

"Well," she had begun, sounding hesitant, "it's, um, one of the three essentials, along with salt and mercury, and it's represented with a runic mark of a double cross rising out of a sideways figure eight, for, um, for infinity, I suppose. Is that a sufficient answer, sir?"

"I'm aghast," the teacher had said. "Would you like to go on?"

"Well, sulfur and mercury are associated with the fire element, and when catalyzed by salt, which represents the earth element, they can at least theoretically form a stone that turns lesser metals into gold. I've found that pink salts from an inland sea such as the Gozo Lagoon in Malta work quite well as a catalyst, but I made only a small amount of gold when I tried and my stone was unstable. Still, that's considered advanced for student work, at least that's what the teacher said. Are we going to try to make g—what's the matter?" Sie had paused to look around the room. Students were laughing.

"We are *definitely not* going to make *gold*." The teacher's tone was acid. "*You* are going to *detention*. And next time, if you don't know the answer, admit it! I can't stand it when students make up ridiculous answers." And then he had rambled on about the periodic table of the elements, while Sie, her back very straight, tried to ignore the persisting whispers and giggles.

Raahi had been intrigued. He'd read widely enough to know that her answer had been correct—at least, for an alchemist. But why had she been studying alchemy instead of modern chemistry? He wanted to speak to her about it, but after class she rushed away. Then school had ended for the summer, and he'd never gotten the chance.

He was reading, as usual, when he heard a screeching of brakes as a yellow taxi stopped outside his apartment. He looked up and thought he saw the same girl get out of the cab. She seemed to be carrying a large birdcage. Hurrying to the window, he watched her go down the sidewalk and through the gate of a house a few doors away from his. (He lived in the first floor apartment in the rear of a large house that had been converted to apartments by floor.) His eyesight sometimes tricked him, so he decided to go outside and see if it really was her.

He hurried past the several intervening doorways to where he thought she had gone in. There he stood, looking up at the rear windows of the house, a frown on his face, wondering whether she could possibly be on his block. He was pretty sure that the house was occupied by that loud family of boys. The older ones, triplets, used to cuff him on the head and steal his glasses on the school bus. Yes, he was quite certain it was their house. He usually avoided it.

It was getting dark and the house looked deserted. Raahi shrugged and went back into his apartment, where his mother was just serving dinner. But the next morning, after they had cleared the breakfast dishes and his mother had gone off to work, he went back out and stood by the fence, studying that house again. Had he really seen her, or was it just someone who reminded him of her? His vision was so annoyingly unreliable. Unless people were directly in the narrow central portion of his field of view, they were so dim and fuzzy that he sometimes missed them entirely.

His mind ran on to the next obvious question: If it had really been her, why had she been carrying a birdcage? The whole thing seemed so unlikely in the bright, sunny light of morning that he began to doubt himself. He polished his glasses thoughtfully, put them back on, sighed, and was just turning away when the door popped open and Sie reappeared.

She leaned down, extracted a key from beneath a flowerpot, locked the door, and returned the key to its position beneath the pot. Then she came down the stairs and paused in front of him. He was blocking her way.

"Uh, excuse me. I, I, wanted to, uh, ask you about alchemy," he ad-libbed as she squeezed around him.

She took a few hurried steps, then paused and turned around, eyeing him with deep suspicion. "You want to tease me about that chemistry class, don't you?" she demanded. "You were there."

"Yes. I mean, no! I was there but I didn't laugh. I've read about alchemy. Your answer was correct. Have you really *done* alchemy?" he hurried to add as she turned and headed off down the sidewalk.

She did not answer. She was already several yards ahead and seemed eager to increase the distance between them.

"Hold on, please," he managed to huff. His breath was already short from trying to keep pace with her. "My asthma acts up in hot weather. Could I just talk to you? Huff. Huff. Please?"

She stopped and turned around. "Asthma? Oh." Her expression softened. "My aunt had that. Have you tried . . ." She let her sentence trail off, as if afraid of embarrassing herself again.

"Tried what?" he asked, and he must have sounded sincerely interested, because she took a step toward him and raised her hand.

"This won't hurt. At least, I don't think so," she said. Then she recited something rapidly in what sounded to him like ancient Latin.

A gust of cool wind struck him in the chest and face and he was pushed back so hard by it that he stumbled and sat down awkwardly on the cement sidewalk. Everything went blurry and his head spun. There was a hot rush of eager blood racing through his body. His skin tingled.

Then the odd feelings subsided and he hurried to get back onto his feet.

He took a deep, steady breath. He let it out. He waited a moment, then took another. His breathing was fine. Excellent, actually. No wheezing. Lots of fresh oxygen flooding in. He felt . . . great! He wanted to ask her what she had done, but she was gone.

However, this gets us ahead of Sie's experiences that morning. Let's go back and follow her until we catch up.

CHAPTER 6

Modern Shopping

Sie stood in the messy kitchen, thinking intently. How would she get food over the summer? She knew she'd have to buy it with green paper bills and small copper and silver coins. She'd seen some of them in her month here in the modern world, but they didn't look familiar. *And that could be a problem,* she thought. *A big problem.*

She jogged upstairs and went through her purse. It held a one-dollar paper note with a black eagle in the middle of it, an oversized ten-dollar bill with a bison, and a gold two-and-a half-dollar coin. Setting those aside, she examined the smaller coins and frowned. She was pretty sure this world didn't have two-cent coins or any pennies with flying eagles on them. None of her money would be familiar to a clerk at a store. (She'd grabbed the little purse in a hurry and stuffed it in her bag the weekend her mother had brought her here but had yet to come up with any way to actually shop with what was in it.) Frustrated, she tossed the purse onto her bed.

She went back downstairs, still thinking. The cousins shopped regularly: big boxes of Choco-Monster Puffs and Marshmallow Chocolate Chip Bars for the boys, along with granola and salad greens and flank steaks for the parents. So many colorful boxes would come back from those shopping trips, most of them frozen and kept in the electric icebox. Sie did not understand why they so seldom ate any fresh food. Auntie used to send her out each day for a fresh fish or some newly cut chops from the local markets. But regardless, they *must* keep money around for their shopping . . .

No, she thought, *they use those strange plastic cards. And I know where they keep the one they use for groceries!*

She slid open a kitchen drawer and there, in a shallow bowl with a pile of receipts and losing lottery tickets, was a green plastic card with some bank's name on it and an embedded gold "chip" of some sort. She vaguely recalled from the only time she'd been taken shopping that the chip could "talk" to a little box at the store and tell it to take money from the cousins' bank. She smiled and slipped the card in her pocket. A moment later, she had locked the kitchen door behind her and was hurrying down the back steps toward the alley.

Her way was blocked by a boy about her age, with dark hair, thick glasses over a long nose, and an expression that mixed surprise with embarrassment. He looked vaguely familiar, but she could not recall why. Frowning, she squeezed past him and headed up the alley in the direction of the nearest convenience store.

That was when he asked her something about alchemy.

When, a moment later, she had hurried away from him and turned the corner to make sure she was out of sight, she shook her head and muttered, "That was stupid of me! Auntie said never to use a spell here." It was strictly forbidden.

"Leave your spells at the side door," she'd tell Sie with a wink. "Although I don't mind helping you with homework, of course," she sometimes added. But they only discussed wards and weavings and workings in the privacy of their parlor. Never out and about in the front-door world, where someone might hear. And now she had gone and done a fairly major working on a strange boy. What had she been thinking! But he'd reminded her of how Aunt Gen would sometimes get short of breath and ask Sie to do an opening chant to let the air into her lungs properly again. It had been a natural response to hearing someone wheeze like Auntie used to. She'd not even thought; she'd just made the sign with her hands to call oxygen to her and then spoken the words of the working.

"Are you going to pay?" It was the clerk, a tall, thin man who hadn't shaved for a few days, glaring down at her.

"Oh. Sorry. I was thinking." She hurried to pull the card out of a pocket and slide it into the strange reader thingy. A bright glass screen told her not to remove her card. Then it told her to take the card and Sign Here.

"Where?" she asked, looking puzzled. There was no pen, nor any paper.

The man arched an eyebrow. "Where have you been all your life? You must be the only teenager who doesn't know how to use a card reader."

Sie did not know what to say to that.

The man pointed a long, pasty finger at the little lit screen. "Right there. Use your finger."

She scrawled her aunt's name as best she could, watching the line magically appear as her finger traced across the glass: F. Lee Jones. (Her Uncle, Randal Jones, was not from the family. Aunt Foolish had married him at a young age and promptly switched to their family name, Lee, as a stand-in for her first name, abbreviating Foolish to F. Sie did not blame her. Imagine how much teasing she must have gotten when *she* was in school!)

The screen blinked, then a long, thin tongue of paper spat out of another machine and the tall man tore it off and handed it to her. "Thanks for shopping at CornerMart," he muttered.

She hurried off, shopping bag firmly gripped in one hand, the other busy stuffing the card back into her pocket. As she shouldered her way out the swinging glass door to the sidewalk, she bumped into a boy who was coming toward her, his arm out as if reaching to push the door open. He didn't seem to see her. His hand bumped into her bag. It was the boy with the very thick glasses.

The bag slipped and fell to the sidewalk. Apples rolled away, and a crunching sound told her that the jar of strawberry jam she'd bought, to have with the loaf of bread she'd also bought, was now quite broken. "You idiot!" she snapped, glaring at him. "What do you think you're doing?"

He looked mortified. "I'm sorry! I, I didn't, I mean, I wasn't, um, well, okay, I was following you, but I didn't mean to bump into you, I swear! I'm just kind of clumsy, you see, because . . ." He took the thick glasses off and began to polish them nervously on the tail of his shirt. It was, she was surprised to note, a rather old-fashioned cotton dress shirt, light blue, neatly ironed, but untucked and falling over a pair of cutoff khakis that were beginning to fray where he had amateurishly converted them to shorts with (she guessed) a dull pair of scissors.

She was still scowling as she bent over to pick up the apples.

"Oh no! Your jam! I'll, I'll . . ." He did not actually seem to know what he would do.

"Go get me another bag. I'll have to throw this one away." She extracted the loaf of bread, which had glass chips from the jam jar stuck to it. She gave it a wipe with the shopping bag, then dropped the shopping bag and the broken jam jar into a trash can that stood just outside the door to the shop.

"Okay," he said, and he hurried into the store.

She did not wait for him. Instead, she opened the plastic bag that held the bread and stuffed her apples into it too. Then she stormed off down the sidewalk, startling a little old lady with three poodles as she leaped over the tangle of leashes and rushed past. The dogs were still barking when she reached the end of the block and hurried around the corner and out of sight.

She arrived, rather breathless, at the cousins' back door again. She was just leaning over to extract the hidden key from beneath the flowerpot when a loud "Caw! Caw!" interrupted her. She looked up, gasped, and ducked, throwing an arm over her head just in time to miss being struck by a crow. It swooped away and landed on the roof of the house next door, where it perched, eyeing her.

"What's the matter with you!" she shouted at it.

"I'm very sorry. I'm not following you, not this time. I'm just walking home." The boy was there again, out on the sidewalk by the gate. He pointed down the street.

"You live here?" She stared at him.

"Actually, yes, I do. Is that a problem?"

"I hope not," Sie said with a frown. "Did you see that crow?"

"No, but I heard it. Why?"

"Never mind." She turned and unlocked the door. Then she paused, hesitant to return the key to its hiding place while the boy was watching her. "Are you going home now?" she asked.

"Me? Of course. I was just passing by." However, he seemed reluctant to leave.

"I'm waiting," Sie said, scowling at him.

"Okay, bye. But I do hope to—Arey!" He ducked and covered his head. The crow had just dived off the rooftop, swishing low and nearly pecking him.

"Watch out!" Sie called. The crow was circling around and coming at him.

One arm protectively covering his head, hunched over, he rushed forward with the crow driving him from behind. He stumbled around the rusty gate. With the crow chasing him the whole way, he rushed up the walk and leaped up the steps toward where Sie was standing on the little landing by the kitchen door.

Sie pushed the door open, and, backing up hastily, pulled the boy in. As she slammed it shut, they could hear the crow slap into it. There was another angry caw and then silence.

They stood on the edge of the kitchen, panting.

Silent's composure returned first. She flipped on the overhead lights, stepped over to the island, and set down what was left of her shopping. She took her cardigan off. She frowned at the messy pizza boxes and piled them on top of the overflowing trash can. Then she turned toward the boy. "Well?" she demanded.

"Don't look at me," he said. "It's not *my* crow."

"Who are you?" She demanded, glaring at him.

"Oh, sorry! I'm Raahi. 'Rah-hee.' From your science class. I live three houses down. I, uh, recognized you."

"Of course you did. I kind of stuck out, didn't I?"

"Well, yes. But not in a bad way." He frowned.

"You've heard of alchemy?" she asked, eyeing him narrowly.

"I read a lot." He shrugged.

"I see." She studied him for a moment. "I think the crow's gone now."

"Oh! Of course. Well, thanks for your help. Enjoy your, um, actually, I guess it won't be a jam sandwich. Can I bring you some jam? We must have some. Or chutney. Do you eat chutney?"

"No thanks."

"Well, I'll just be going then. Uh, goodbye."

"Don't talk about the air-weaving to anyone. No one!"

"Right. Thank you for that. I, I haven't breathed this easily in, um, well, ever. How did—"

"Hey! What part of 'Don't talk to anyone' did you fail to understand?" Sie glared at him.

"Didn't know that included you. Sorry. Um . . . right."

She continued to eye him suspiciously as he backed toward the door, opened it, and disappeared outside.

She went over and turned the latch. "What a strange boy," she muttered. "And what a strange crow!" She shrugged and went back to the kitchen island to unpack her groceries. Her stomach was grumbling with hunger. She'd missed dinner the previous evening, and now it was rather late for breakfast. She slipped two pieces of bread into the toaster and took a tentative bite of one of the bruised apples.

That was when bird song caught her ear. It was coming from the staircase. She put the apple down and hurried into the hall. Yes, it was definitely coming from upstairs.

She took the steps two at a time and rushed down the hall to where the door to the attic was ajar. Her heart racing, she scrambled up the attic stairs and paused at the top, peering into the dim space with its rough old dark wood rafters sweeping down to meet the floor on either side.

The birdcage was sitting in the middle of the room beside her sleeping bag. A rectangle of sunlight filtered in through the attic window and illuminated the cage brightly. In the cage was a lushly leafed branch, and on the branch was perched an amazing blue finch.

The finch turned to study her. She tiptoed over, and it hopped to the end of the branch and stuck its bill through a gap in the wire. It was holding a thin strip of paper. The paper had something written on it, and the handwriting was strangely familiar: A careful block print done with a fountain pen of the kind Aunt Gen used to use. In fact, the writing looked exactly like Aunt Gen's. Not her everyday scrawl, which was a looping cursive, but her printed writing from when she was trying to be neat.

The bird let go of the paper and it fluttered to the attic floor.

Sie picked it up. This is what she read: "Help! I'm a captive at"

The original message must have been longer, but the paper was torn and that was all there was for Sie to see.

Sie's hand shook as she stared at the message. "Auntie, is this from you?" she whispered.

The bird cocked its head and stared at her.

"Where did you get this?" she asked it.

The bird hopped toward the middle of the branch. It flapped down to a lower branch and continued to work its way downward until it had disappeared somewhere beneath the bottom of the birdcage, and there was nothing left to see but shiny green foliage and a little blue butterfly.

The butterfly circled the cage once, then landed and folded its wings, revealing a soft green underside matched so well with the foliage that when Silent looked away, although just for a second, she could not find it again.

She waited for quite some time, but the finch did not come back.

CHAPTER 7

Raahi Investigates

The photocopied list of classmates from eighth grade was folded in half and stuck in the back of a dictionary. Raahi remembered putting it there. But *which* dictionary? Unlike most fourteen-year-old boys, he had many dictionaries.

His current favorites were *The Oxford Dictionary of Etymology* (which told the story of where words came from), and the massive third (and final) edition of the *OED* itself, which was the definitive and best dictionary of the English language. It was so big that it needed its own side table in his already crowded bedroom. He'd found the dictionary, nearly new, in a recycling bin a few years ago. And of course he had foreign-language dictionaries: English-Latin, English-French, English-German, and his latest find, an old Anglo-Hindi dictionary dating from 1938 and labeled on the cover "Hindustani Book Depot, Lucknow." Although his mother was from India, he had grown up in Boston and did not know as much Hindi as he wished to.

Raahi collected his books from recycling bins and tag sales beside the big old houses of Back Bay. *In the old days, people must have had fine libraries in those fine houses,* he thought. Now they were getting rid of the books. He just wished he had more room. His little bedroom was already stacked with heavy volumes.

He was distracted briefly by a dictionary of medical terms. He skimmed the entry on asthma, but there was nothing about a chant to cure the symptoms. How *had* she done that? It was almost like magic.

Thinking about her reminded him he wanted to look up her name on the class list. *Where* had he put the darn thing?

Then a thought stopped him from searching any further. The list had been printed at the beginning of the fall semester, but *she* had joined the class in late spring. She would not be on the list. But she *would* be in the school's latest records, and he thought he knew how to access those.

He put on his best walking shoes, a nearly new pair of high topped sneakers from the Salvation Army Thrift Store on Washington Street. He stuffed a bottle of water and some crackers into his backpack. He paused to grab a novel for reading on the subway, then headed out. "Oops," he said, turning back before he was all the way out the door. "Almost forgot."

He went back in and got his Blind Access Card for the MBTA, which allowed him to ride the subways all over Boston for free. He wasn't "completely blind," as he put it to himself, at least not yet. The distinction was important to him because he so loved to read. However, he suffered from severe tunnel vision, being able to see clearly only in a small circle directly ahead. The rest was murky, at best, which explained his tendency to bump into people. And it was why he qualified for the card.

Leaving his apartment, he turned right and walked to the end of the block, where a narrow park crossed the road. Entering the park, he turned right again and continued past community vegetable gardens and playgrounds until he came to Dartmouth Street. He found the arched entry to the Back Bay T Station, slid his pass through the reader, and went downstairs to wait for the next train on the Orange Line north.

It made a terrific screeching as it came to a stop. The doors banged open, and he got on. He took the nearest seat and began to read his book (Nathaniel Hawthorne's 1851 novel, *The House of the Seven Gables*): "Half-way down a by-street of one of our New England towns stands a rusty wooden house, with seven acutely peaked gables, facing towards various points of the compass, and a huge, clustered chimney in the midst." He frowned and paused to wonder how a wooden house could look rusty and also how a sentence could have so many commas, then he shrugged and returned to his reading. However, he was still struggling through the first page when he had to put it away. The train was pulling into the next station, Tufts Medical Center. From there, it was a only a block and a half to his old school.

He found his way to the office. Even though it was summer vacation, one of the secretaries was there. He was in luck: it was May, the friendliest one. She looked up and gave him a big smile. "Hello, Raahi! What are you doing here?"

"Hi! I just couldn't stay away. Actually, my student directory is from last fall. Can you give me an updated list of my old classmates?"

"We don't redo it for graduating classes."

"I was hoping to get the final list for my class. Do you have the changes from last semester?"

"Why the interest in your class list?"

"I was curious about, um, changes to the list." He thought he must have sounded embarrassed.

May got up from her desk and came over to lean on the counter in front of him. "A long way to come to satisfy your curiosity. Hmm. Well, let's see . . ." She reached under the counter, pulled up a folder, and opened it. "Here's my working list from last semester. Several people left before the end of the school year. Would you like their—"

"I was thinking about new people," he admitted, looking away.

"New students? I think two boys came to us from . . ." She paused when he seemed disinterested. "Not a new boy?" she asked.

He shook his head.

She smiled. "The new girl, then. Let's see . . . yes, her last name was Lee. I remember that much." May ran her finger through the list. "I'd expected she'd be Korean or Chinese with a name like that, but she turned out to be from England, I think? I didn't get to know her."

No one did, Raahi thought. He guessed May was recalling the girl's old-fashioned clothing and otherworldly air. And her speech was far too proper and articulate to sound like a typical kid from Boston. Raahi had been to London to visit relatives, and he did not think she had a British accent, but he could see how they might have guessed she was from the UK. Not American, anyway.

"That's her," he said.

May smiled. "I suppose you'd like to know her name and contact information?"

He nodded. "She's a new neighbor, and I'm embarrassed I don't remember her name. I, uh, bumped into her this morning."

"I see." She smiled again. "I don't see any harm in telling you that since she would've been on your class list handout if she'd been here all along. Her name, according to this, is . . . wait, this must be a typo."

"What?"

"It says her name is Silent. Silent Lee. Do you suppose that's someone's idea of a joke?" May looked annoyed.

"I don't know. Is her address on Yarmouth Street?"

"Newbury. No, wait, that was the first address we were given, but she moved to Yarmouth to stay with a family by the name of Jones."

"Her cousins," Raahi said. "The younger twins go here and the older triplets used to."

"Goodness! The poor girl." May frowned. "Some of the worst be-haved students we've ever had."

"That's them," Raahi said. "They used to steal my glasses on the school bus."

"I'm not surprised. They spent a lot of time in detention. I hope Silent proves nicer than the rest of that family. It would be fun to have a friend on your block." She smiled again.

"Yes. Um, thanks. It was great to see you." He turned and bumped into a locked door. The office had double doors, one of the pair being open and the other firmly latched. "Oops! Uh, bye." He made his way out and started back toward the T station, but then decided to walk. It would give him time to think about what his research had revealed: The girl's name was Silent. Silent Lee. Or else someone had hacked the school's files and changed it as a joke. But that seemed like a lot of trouble. The jokes made by eighth—soon to be ninth—graders, were usually much simpler and more crude. Probably her name really *was* Silent. In a way, it fit her. She rarely said anything. But what she did say, on the few occasions he'd heard her speak, was remarkable.

He was curious about the city's layout and often studied an old street map he'd found, so it was a simple matter for him to choose a walking route home. The Josiah Quincy School was on Washington Street. Turning left and left again, he walked down Oak, which soon became Tremont and veered southward to cross over the highway. A right onto Appleton took him three blocks over to Dartmouth Street. He headed north on Dartmouth past the French Cleaners; its distinct smell of cleaning solvents told him he was nearing home. Yarmouth Street was behind Dartmouth but screened by tall brick buildings and thick trees, so he went a block past and turned left onto the Southwest Corridor Path, where his journey to the T had started that morning. On his old map it was a trolley line, but now it had been made into a long, thin park.

From there, it was an easy several minutes to get to his apartment, where his mother would be home for lunch and expecting him. Leftovers, he imagined: They'd had fluffy white rice and butter chicken last night, tenderly tossed in an aromatic, creamy red sauce. His mother was an excellent cook and he was pleased to be on time for the hot lunch he assumed she was preparing. His trip had timed out just as he'd planned.

What he had *not* planned on was being attacked by crows again.

CHAPTER 8

Questions

Silent had taken her strange slip of paper to the attic window to study it in the light, but the window was so old and wavy and dusty and small that she decided to go downstairs and look at it in the sunlight on the back porch.

She stopped briefly to put some bread in the toaster (it was time for lunch, and all she had was bread, so toast would have to do). Then she rummaged through the kitchen drawers. She thought she'd seen a magnifying glass somewhere, but now she couldn't find it.

Shrugging, she stepped out into the sunlight and stretched the strip of paper out. The writing really did seem to be Auntie's. But how could Auntie be a captive? They told her . . . Sie frowned. Yes, they'd been very specific and clear about it. She was dead. There'd even been a memorial service. The cousins and Sie's mother had been there, and some of the neighbors, older men and women who had known Aunt Gen for many years. And the strange men in dark suits, watching them from the back of the little stone chapel beside Emmanuel Church, which was only a few blocks away from Auntie's cozy house. Sie frowned. There was even a stone with Auntie's name on it in a cemetery, across the river somewhere Sie had never been before or since, with lots of trees and bushes—Mount Auburn, she thought it had been called. (And she'd thought she'd spotted more men in dark suits and dark glasses in the distance at the cemetery that day, too . . .)

The thing is, she thought, *I didn't actually see her . . . I wasn't there when . . .* Auntie had been in bed with a cold when Mother had come up and taken Sie with her to stay a whole weekend at a hotel (that had never happened before). Then Mother had dropped Sie at the cousins' instead of Auntie's. Later, Mother had come back with the news that Auntie had died. Now Sie had to ask herself a difficult question: Did she believe her mother?

She was thinking very hard about this question, which was a troubling one because there was little reason, she realized, to consider her mother trustworthy. She did not even know for sure what her mother's job was or where she went when she was gone.

Sie's thoughts were interrupted by a commotion up the block.

A crow cawed loudly. And another and another.

Someone shouted, "Hey! Go away!"

It was that boy. He was running down the sidewalk toward her. A whole flock of crows was flapping after him.

Sie pointed her forefinger at him and muttered a warding. It was a spell from her studies at GALA, and it was effective against just about any animal attack.

The crows sounded quite annoyed as they swooped off and perched in a sidewalk tree.

"Oh! That's much better. Thank you." The boy came up the little path toward her. "What did you do?"

Sie's frown deepened. Somehow she'd broken Auntie's rule twice in a row and for the same front-door person. Why was this boy so annoying? And why was he being chased by crows?

"You don't have to tell me if you don't want to," he said. "But thanks anyway! You're, um, Silent, aren't you?"

"I don't talk much."

"No, I mean, your name. Is that right?"

She shrugged. "People call me Sie. For short. Bye." She turned and tried to open the kitchen door. It was locked. She glared at him again.

"Uh, I already know the key's beneath the flowerpot," he said. "But I won't tell anyone. So no harm letting yourself in, if you see what I mean."

She glared at him some more. Although he was a little taller, she had the advantage of being higher where she stood on the landing by the kitchen door. She hoped her glare was intimidating enough to send him away.

"My name's—" he began, but she interrupted him.

"Raahi, yes," she snapped. "I know. So why don't you go on about your travels and leave me be?"

"Hah! You know what my name means! Traveler. Very good. Have you studied Hindi?"

"And *my* name means I don't want to talk." She had extracted the key and gotten it into the lock. With an angry turn, she threw the door open and disappeared inside, taking the key with her.

"Of course I know Hindi," she muttered to herself and hurried to take out her overdone toast. "It's one of the fundamental languages of sorcery. And if I were still at my proper school, I wouldn't have to deal with stupid boys who have no idea . . ." She stopped talking. What was the point? No one was listening. No one ever listened, now that Aunt Gen was gone.

"Darn! There's no more butter, and that boy ruined my jam!" She studied the hard, over-browned slices for a moment, then dropped them into the trash bin.

A noise made her turn her head. "Unbelievable!" she spat, again talking to herself, as the knob turned and the door began to creak open. It was that boy. Again.

"Um, *really* sorry to bother you, but . . ." He came in a step or two, leaving the door ajar behind him and squinting around the kitchen uncertainly.

"But *what*?" Sie demanded.

"Oh, there you are. So much darker inside," he said dismissively, as if self-conscious about his uncertainty. "Um, one of the crows . . ." He paused.

"They won't bother you now. Go away."

"Yes, I mean, I will, but . . . say, it smells like burnt toast. I'm sorry I broke your jar of chutney. Do you—"

"Strawberry jam. My favorite." She was working her glare again, but it did not seem to be having its usual effect. It occurred to her that he might not be able to see it clearly. She came toward him.

"Strawberry, yes, sorry about that. My mum's making lunch, you know, and I'm sure she'd be happy to meet you and all that. You being a neighbor now," he hastened to explain. "She's kind of old fashioned and believes in being friendly to neighbors," he added. "So if you don't have anything but burnt toast for lunch, why don't you—"

"You broke in just to invite me to lunch?" Sie's sarcasm was unmistakable, even if her deep scowl was hard for him to read in the dimmer light of the kitchen.

"No! Well, yes, but . . ." He fumbled in a pocket. "I also came to show you this." He had a thin, wrinkled strip of paper in his hand with old-fashioned block lettering running along it.

"I'll take that," Sie snapped, reaching out and grabbing it. "Where in the world did you get it?"

"The crows. They seemed to be trying to give it to me. After you did, um, whatever you did to keep them away, one of them dropped this from its perch in a tree above me. It fluttered right past my face and into my hand. I actually caught it as it fell."

"So what? It's none of your business. Goodbye."

"I never catch anything. I can't really see well enough for that. So I think it was *meant* for me. As strange as it sounds, I think the crows somehow made sure I got it. In fact, they probably weren't attacking me, actually. Just trying to give this to me. Does it mean something to you? I thought, you know, that it might."

"Why?" She was suddenly suspicious of him. "What do you know?"

He shrugged. "I just know that if it seems like too many coincidences, it probably is."

"Explain."

"Well, first I bumped into you."

"That wasn't a coincidence. You were following me!"

"Sorry about that, but you *did* appear here on my block. And then I really *did* bump into you by accident at the store. Add now two separate attacks by crows, both when you're nearby."

She frowned. "I see what you mean. Darn!"

"What's the matter?"

"I have a lot to think about already. And now, you."

"I don't mean to be any trouble."

"But you are." She turned and set his slip of paper down on the kitchen island, next to hers. "Do you know what happened to my aunt?"

"Have they disappeared? The, um, loud boys and their parents?"

"No, of course not. Well, actually, yes, but I don't care about them. I mean my great aunt. Do you have any information about her, anything at all?"

"From Newbury Street?"

She spun around. "How did you know that?" she demanded.

He looked embarrassed.

"Well?"

"I'm sorry. Don't be mad. Please?"

"What did you do?" She was almost shouting at him now.

He backed away, swung the door open, and retreated to the landing outside. The sun was bright there. He blinked awkwardly in its glare. "It's just, I was curious, you know. I mean, after we, um, bumped into each other. About your, um, name. I didn't have anything else to do, so I went to school and, um, looked you up."

"You went to that school in Chinatown just to find out my name?" She stared at him, startled at the ridiculousness of the thought. "Why?"

"And you had two addresses listed. The older one's on Newbury Street, so I assumed that must be where this aunt person you're talking about lived."

"You've been spying on me!" She came to the kitchen door and took a firm grip on the handle. "Why?"

"I'm sorry . . . I . . . I . . ." He seemed very embarrassed.

"Why?"

"Well, I suppose," he stammered, looking down at his sneakers, "that, um, I might have had just a very small, you know, a minor, well, a bit of a crush on you. Nothing serious!" he added quickly. "And I'm sure it will pass. It probably has already. Yes, I think so, almost certainly, but . . ."

She stared at him for a long moment, and then she began to laugh.

CHAPTER 9

Curried Chicken

Sie thought Raahi's explanation was quite funny. *Very* funny, actually. He'd gone all the way to school, when the school bus wasn't running, just to find out her name because he had a *crush* on her? The idea of anyone having a crush on her seemed ridiculous. And that he would actually admit it . . . what a funny character he was! But he did seem to be intelligent, and at least he didn't make fun of her.

She stopped laughing. There was something much more important to consider. The notes. And Auntie. What had the crow's note said? She turned back to where she'd laid the two side by side and read out loud, "Help! I'm a captive at . . . ext door to Mr. Vo . . . e's art. Silent, he has a side door too."

"See? Definitely written for you," Raahi said. "That's why I—"

"Shh. I'm thinking."

"Sorry. What does 'next door to—'"

"*Shhh!*"

"Right." He stood quietly, watching her.

After a long moment, she turned to him and said, "I can't think properly when you're staring at me."

"I'm not staring. Well, technically, I suppose I am, since I can only focus on one specific spot in the middle of my field of vi—"

"Do you mind?"

"I can just look out the window if you want."

"Do that." She frowned and stared at the message for a long time. "Is it from your—"

"Please! Yes. It must be. But . . ." She stared at it some more. "Who would take her captive? And why lie to me about her being dead?"

"She's not dead?"

"Of course not! I don't think so, anyway. She's captive. See?"

Raahi came over to squint at the notes. "That's good news, isn't it?" he asked.

"Definitely. But that means my mother lied to me. Of course she's a spy and her entire life is probably a lie, but why lie about *that?*"

"A spy? Uh, is there someone else you can ask? Someone you trust?"

Sie was silent for some time. Finally she shook her head. Raahi didn't seem to notice. "No," she said quietly. "No one. Unless . . ."

"Unless what?"

"Unless I can get back to, well, to my old school."

"I know the city quite well. Where is it?"

"Dartmouth and Commonwealth, but it's not there now." She gazed thoughtfully out the window. "It's complicated."

"Is everything complicated with you?"

Sie sighed. "Actually, yes. But it's not your problem. Thanks for the note."

"You're sending me away again, right?" he asked.

She nodded, but he was staring at the note. "Who is Mr. Vo?" he asked.

"I don't know. The crow's beak messed up the paper. I think there's supposed to be more letters."

"Now you mention it," he said, rubbing his finger gently over the spot, "I think it might say V-O-S-E."

"Vose? Yes! That's Auntie's friend, the art dealer."

"There's a building with that name on its sign," Raahi said. "On Newbury Street. Vose Gallery. Right?"

"Yes. But Mr. Vose is . . . well, he's probably not there anymore. He was a very *old* friend." (He was from the side-door world, and Silent doubted he would be here in this world.)

"What does this mean about a side door?" Raahi persisted.

"Hmm." Silent thought some more. "Maybe a way to reach my school and find someone who can help. And definitely a clue as to where my aunt is. I've got to go there." Silent looked up. "Now."

"Oh yes! We should go right away." Raahi looked excited. "I love adventures!"

"Not you. Sorry."

"But, well, at least have lunch before you go."

Sie meant to refuse. She normally would have, but her stomach gave a tremendous grumble and she realized she was very hungry. What harm would it do to grab a quick bite to eat? And that way, she could make sure Raahi was deposited safely at home before she went off in search of Aunt Gen. "Okay," she said. "But I don't have much time."

Feeling awkward, Sie allowed herself to be lead to Raahi's apartment (which was at sidewalk level, with his mother's herb garden outside the door). They hurried to the door and Raahi pulled out a key to let them in. "Maa? Hello? Maa? I brought . . ." He paused and cocked his head to listen. "That's funny. I wonder where she is."

"There's a note on the table," Sie pointed out.

He went over to the kitchen table, picked it up, and brought it to the light of the window above the kitchen sink. "Oh. She's helping the old lady who lives upstairs with her shopping trip. She's left food for me. Well, us. We can share it. She always leaves a lot." He smiled.

"That's all right," Sie said. "I really need to—"

"Please, sit down." He went to the table again and lifted lids off.

An aromatic smell wafted up from something orange in one dish. The other held steaming rice. "See?"

"Well—" Sie approached nose first.

"Here." He heaped rice and curried chicken into a bowl and handed it to her with a spoon. "Have some before we go."

"Mmm! Delicious." She took several more bites. "This is really good."

"Sit down. I'll get you some tea, if you can wait long enough for the kettle to boil? No. Then how about a glass of chhachh. Uh, buttermilk."

"N-no thanks."

"Then at least a glass of water. Here." He hurried to fill a small glass at the sink. "Straight from the Quabbin Reservoir, you know. Way out in the western part of the state and surrounded by forest. Very pure! Boston is lucky to have such good . . . sorry, I shouldn't talk so much."

"No, you shouldn't," she said. "But thanks. I was starved."

"No need to wash your bowl," he hurried to say as she turned on the kitchen tap. "I'll clean up later. Now we will follow the clue." He took another bite out of the bowl he'd prepared for himself, then set it down. "Are you ready?"

Sie studied him for a moment. "Look," she said, "I can't bring you with me. It's hard to explain."

"But I'm already involved," he objected. "Obviously, your Great Aunt Gin—"

"Gen!"

"She wants me to help you, or why send the crows to me instead of you? It must have been her, since they carried her message, right?"

Sie frowned more deeply. "I suppose so. It hardly seems like chance. Too many coincidences, like you said. But why include you?"

"Why indeed?" He smiled. "We shall soon find out!"

"Sorry, but I can't take you where I'm going. Thanks for lunch, though."

"Because your Aunt Gen is a famous witch or wizard or something like that, and you are studying with her in secret? See, I already know you can do magic and even a little alchemy. So, what's there to keep secret?"

Sie raised an eyebrow. "You have no idea. But . . ." She recalled that he'd gotten half of the note. "I suppose you can at least come check out the gallery and whatever's next door. The note says she's being kept near it, right?"

"Right. Do you have the note?"

"It's on the kitchen counter. We can stop and get it on the way."

And that was how, quite to Sie's surprise, she found herself heading out the door with Raahi, a strange boy she'd only just met, instead of going to search for her aunt all by herself.

CHAPTER 10

The Annoying Strangers

They hurried down the sidewalk but stopped when they reached the rear gate. From there, they could see strangers gathered at the cousins' back door. A tall man in a Yankees baseball cap was holding a suitcase in his hand. A short, rather stout woman was just leaning over to look beneath the flowerpot for the key. (Sie had returned it to its usual place when they went out.) An older woman with white hair and numerous wrinkles was standing at the bottom of the stairs as if waiting for someone to come and help her up. Two boys in their early teens and a girl in her late teens were on the sidewalk, large suitcases in tow.

"Arey!" Raahi's exclamation of surprise had come out in Hindi. While he rarely spoke the language with anyone but his mother, he tended to revert to it when startled, and this was a very startling sight.

Sie said, "What the—? Wait here!" She pushed through the gate and up the path, squeezing past the larger children and their big suitcases, until she was standing next to the old woman at the bottom of the steps. "May I help you?" she demanded.

The old woman looked flustered.

"Don't bother my mother," the man barked, scowling down at Sie.

Sie ignored the man and addressed the other woman, who was just opening the kitchen door. "Uh, what do you think you're doing?"

"Honey, would you get rid of that annoying child?" the woman said over her shoulder as she pushed through the door, pulling a very bright pink suitcase with her. "And you'll have to complain to Cheap Rental Experience and Event Planner Dot Con," she added loudly from inside the kitchen. "This place is a mess!"

"It's CREEP-dot-*com*, not *con*, dear," the man said, sounding annoyed. "I've told you that a hundred times."

"Creep? Is that really supposed to make me feel *better?*" the woman complained from within the kitchen.

With shouts of "Where's my bedroom?" and "Me first!" the teenagers pushed past Sie and up the steps, following their mother into the kitchen.

The man put a very heavy and rather hairy hand on Sie's shoulder and said, "Off you go, little girl. We don't like nosey neighbors." Then he pushed her toward the street (she nearly stumbled and fell), turned, and took the old woman by the arm. "Come along, mother. Careful on the steps. This is where we're spending the month. Don't you remember? I told you all about it last night."

"I want to go back home," the old woman said. "I miss my armchair." But she allowed the tall man to guide her through the kitchen door. It swung behind them with a bang.

Sie stood staring at the closed door then turned toward Raahi. He was out by the curb in front of a rather beat-up silver minivan with bumper stickers saying things like, "I climbed Mount Monadnock," "This way to Franconia Notch," and "Life as we know it began on Plymouth Beach."

"They seem to be on a summer vacation," Raahi said. "Did your relatives rent out their house for the summer?"

"I guess so," Sie said, sounding defeated. "Figures." She came back down the walk slowly, her eyes hot with angry tears. "The jerks!"

"They did seem unfriendly," Raahi admitted, "but if someone rented the house to them, it's not really their fault."

"I mean my cousins!" Sie snapped. "And my mother. They . . ." She bit her lower lip.

"They what?" he asked, looking at her with concern.

"They forgot about me. Completely!" She stood up straighter and her eyes flashed with anger. "And I think they did something to my Aunt Generous. Come on, Raahi. I'm going to deal with this *right now!*"

"The note?" he asked as she started off down the sidewalk.

She stopped and turned. "Darn! It's still in the kitchen. I bet that witch'll think it's trash and throw it away."

"Actually, you're the witch, if you don't mind my saying so." Raahi studied her. "Can't you, you know, *do* something?"

She glared at him. *If he could see me clearly,* she thought, *he certainly wouldn't have a crush on me, because I usually look at him like I'd like to wring his neck!* She swung her gaze back to the house. She frowned. A kitchen window was open. Sparrows were twittering in a bush beneath it. "I'm not allowed to . . ."

"It's an emergency," he said. "And the sidewalk's empty. Nobody will see you. I hardly count," he added with a grin, "since I can hardly see."

She closed her eyes and muttered something soft and soothing. The birds stopped twittering and turned their little bright eyes toward her. The link was made. Now she just had to project an image of the slips of paper and the kitchen island through the open window. She visualized everything as fully and accurately as possible, and then held the image for a long minute in which she hardly breathed.

The sparrows twittered again, talking to each other in their own little language.

One flapped up and landed on the windowsill, peeping in. She supposed it was checking for danger. She hoped the people had moved on to explore the rest of the house.

It disappeared inside. Then the rest of the flock followed it through the kitchen window.

Sie and Raahi waited, watching tensely, but nothing happened.

Still nothing.

There was a piercing scream. "Aahhhh! There's filthy ugly birds in here! Get a broom, quick!" It sounded like the woman with the pink suitcase.

Banging noises burst out the kitchen window, followed by grating and smashing sounds, as if the stools at the kitchen island were being pushed over and some of them broken.

Another really loud bang. Sie thought it might have been the broom hitting a kitchen cabinet. She hoped the cabinet door was smashed. It would serve the cousins right. She hoped the birds were *not* smashed. That would be on her. She held her breath and, without thinking, reached over and grabbed Raahi's hand, squeezing it tightly.

Sparrows burst out the window, followed by curses and a broom.

"They're okay," she breathed, very relieved.

"Do they have the note?" Raahi asked. He was squeezing her hand tightly too. It was a tense moment.

"Yes! Here they come!" The little brown birds flapped across the yard, twittering excitedly, and dropped two thin pieces of paper. The papers fluttered down on the sidewalk near Sie's feet.

She let go of Raahi's hand and leaned down. "Got them," she said. She couldn't help feeling somewhat pleased with herself.

"Get out of here, you filthy vermin!" the man shouted. He was leaning out the kitchen window, shaking a large, hairy fist. "And that goes for you too!" he spat, glaring at Sie and Raahi. Then he slammed the kitchen window.

"What about your stuff?" Raahi asked.

"They probably won't go to the attic. There's no light on the staircase and its very spider-webby. Anyway, I hope not."

"You live in an attic?" He looked surprised.

"It's a long story. Anyway, this is all I *really* need," she added as she slipped the pieces of paper into her pocket. "Are you ready?"

"For more excitement and magic? You bet!" Raahi looked positively delighted.

"It's not a game," she said.

"No, of course not. But I'm still having fun." He smiled broadly as they set off down the block, heading north.

"I'm not. But, um, thanks for helping."

CHAPTER 11

Following the Clues

The gallery was easy to find. A set of formal stairs lead up to a large, light-blue doorway in the multistory brick building. Out on the sidewalk, the black ironwork fence had the name VOSE welded into it in gold-painted block letters. Above the arching doorway the street address was displayed: 238. They stood outside, looking up at the somewhat intimidating entry.

"The note," Sie said. "Do you remember exactly what it said?" She rummaged in her pocket.

Raahi beat her to it; he had already committed it to memory. "It said," he offered, "'Help! I'm a captive at . . . next door to Mr. Vose's Art. Silent, he has a side door too.' Once I read something, I tend not to forget it."

Sie glanced at the scraps of paper. "Right," she said. "Okay, what's next door to the gallery?"

At 240, which was at the end of the block, there were a number of establishments: A bank had its ATM there. There was a small drugstore. A modern gallery advertised an art show upstairs.

"I don't see where they'd hide her in there," Sie said. "But I guess we could try to search the building."

"What about on the other side?" Raahi asked.

They walked over to study the building at 236 Newbury. A large, modern sign advertised the Shake Shack on the ground floor. Next to it, stairs lead to a varnished oak door with lots of little window panes in it. People were coming and going through the door, suggesting residences. The people seemed young, hip, and happy. Not evil, as far as Sie could see. Not like those creepy men in the dark suits and dark glasses with the dark tinted windows on their black SUVs. The men who tended to show up whenever her mother was in town. The men who looked like that man over there, glancing up and down the sidewalk suspiciously before walking up a brick path to a sidewalk-level oak and glass door sandwiched inconspicuously between the European Watch Company on the left and outdoor seating for Shake Shack on the right. "What's *that* building?" Sie asked in a whisper.

"It must be number 234," Raahi said.

"That's what it says above the door, but there aren't any signs."

"Signs?" Raahi repeated. "What do you mean?"

"The other buildings have signs telling you what's in them. That one doesn't."

"Interesting. Wait here." He headed up the brick walkway toward the door.

"I'm coming with you," Sie said, hurrying after him.

The door was locked, but they could peek through a narrow window into an ordinary-looking entryway. There was a small brass plaque by the elevator.

"What does it say?" Raahi asked.

"Hold on. Hard to read. Um . . . Global Hospitality Suites. And, um, Oakwood Residencies. And some floor numbers. Four floors, I think. No, if I squint a certain way, there's also a Wormwood Suites, Fifth Floor."

"Residencies and suites." Raahi thought for a moment. "Probably short-term rentals. Like for a month or a week. Not regular apartments."

"It seems so impersonal and anonymous," Sie said. "And that creepy man in the dark suit went in."

"We ought to search it," Raahi said. They had backed up and were standing on the sidewalk, studying the building. "How do we get in?"

"I don't know. It's locked."

"There must be unlocking spells," Raahi said.

"They're strictly disallowed in school. Only criminals use them."

"Doesn't that make them very interesting to students?" Raahi smiled.

"Well . . ."

"Then what are we waiting for?" Before Sie could think of a suitable reply, Raahi had darted back up the brick walk toward the entry. The walk was shaded by the building, and he did not notice the large man in the dark suit and dark glasses hurrying out the door.

They collided in the middle of the walk.

The man looked annoyed but did not break stride as Raahi bounced off and landed on his rear.

Leaving Raahi sprawled on the bricks, the man hurried off down the sidewalk to where a waiting SUV was illegally parked, its warning lights on, waiting. He got in with a slam of a rear door, and the SUV honked and pushed out into the traffic.

Sie hurried to help Raahi up. "Are you all right?"

"We've definitely found our bad guys," Raahi said, rubbing his elbow. "Ow! He's big."

"Why did you—never mind. Is anything broken?"

"I'm all right, *and* . . ." He smiled and waved his hand in the air. He was holding a cell phone. It was thin and black.

"Raahi! You shouldn't have."

"It fell underneath me. Not my fault. But let's take a look, shall we?" He touched the screen. "Excellent! He must've just used it. The security hasn't kicked in yet." Raahi tapped the screen until it displayed a bright list of phone numbers. "It's his call log. He makes lots of calls. Huh. Mostly to the same number."

"It's in the 710 area code," Sie said, looking over his shoulder. "Where's that?"

"Not where," Raahi said. "Who. I was reading about the development of the North American Numbering Plan by AT&T and the US government back in the 1940s, and it's really quite an interesting histor—"

"Raahi!"

"Oh, sorry. The 710 area code is reserved for special government uses. The public can't use it. Which means that your strange man in the dark glasses is working for our government."

"Mother!"

"Your mother? What about her?" Raahi looked confused.

"Auntie always said she worked for the CIA, but *she* said she was a spice importer. I bet those men work with her." Sie looked quite angry.

"Let's see what else is on his phone," Raahi said, lifting it up and tapping the screen again.

There was a bright flash of light and a *click*.

"Hey!" Raahi complained. "It just took my picture!"

"Can you erase it?" Sie asked.

"Delete it? No, the screen's frozen now. See?"

"Don't point it at *me*," Sie complained, ducking.

"Huh. Now it's vibrating on and off, like it's sending out some kind of pulse."

"I don't know about *that* kind of magic," Sie complained.

"Government high tech. Probably not available to the public." He turned the phone over thoughtfully.

"You better put it down," Sie said.

"Right. I'll leave it where I found it." Raahi hurried back up the brick walk and placed the phone on the edge of it, half way under a wide green hosta leaf that was bent and wrinkled from Raahi's re-cent fall. "There. Now we just have to wait and watch. Do you have any money?"

"Me? I hope . . ." She checked her pocket. "Yes! I have the cous-ins' bank card." She showed him.

"It works? Excellent. Let's go to the Shake Shack. We can wait there to see who comes for the phone."

"How will that help?" Sie asked.

"We don't know who his associates are, or how many. For all we know, your mother might show up. 'Know your enemy,' as Master Sun wrote in his fifth century BC Chinese classic, *The Art of War*, although *I* first read a French translation done in the 1700s by—"

"*Raa*hi!"

"Too much information?"

"Way too much. However, it's not a bad idea. The part about watching. *Not* the part about translations of ancient texts." She gave him a stern look.

"The Shake Shack, then," he said happily.

Sie nodded. "It's a good vantage point," she agreed as they headed for the entry, "but are teenagers allowed to buy shakes?"

CHAPTER 12

A Stakeout

Raahi paused to study Sie. "Have you never had a shake?"

"I thought they were, you know, some kind of alcoholic drink served at bars or something," Sie said.

"Maybe they were." Raahi considered. "I haven't read about their history. Yet. But these ones are made of ice cream. Come on, I'll show you. Do you like vanilla, strawberry, or chocolate?"

Sie got a strawberry shake, Raahi vanilla, and they sat at a small, round table by the window. There were open tables on the patio, but they thought they'd be too visible out there.

Sie liked it. It was wonderful to slurp up the thick, icy drink through the straw and feel the sweetness and coldness as it hit her mouth. "Some things about the front door world are all right," she said with a smile.

"Front door world?" Raahi stared at her. "What do you mean?"

"I suppose I'd better explain. It might help us find Aunt Gen. See, as long as you leave her house by the front door, or even a window, you'll end up here in your world, in, um, what year is it?"

"What year is it in *your* world?" Raahi demanded, startled by the thought that it could be different.

"It's about a hundred years different. There are other differences too. You read about history, right?"

"I like to read." He shrugged.

"Clearly." She smiled. "Have you read about Boston a hundred years ago?"

"Oh yes. I go look at old magazines and newspapers sometimes. Have you been to the Boston Public Library?"

"Often, but not in *this* world." She frowned. "I'm not sure it's quite the same. In your history, did they do alchemy?"

"Oh yes. In medieval times, I think. In Europe, a thousand years ago," he added when she looked puzzled.

"Not a hundred years ago in Boston?" she asked.

"No. There were witches around here, though," he added. "In, um, Salem, for instance. It was a few hundred years back. But they were, well, they were . . . hung."

"What are you talking about? Hung from what?"

"From the neck. Witchcraft wasn't allowed."

Sie felt her neck. "That's terrible!"

"In hindsight, people say it was a case of mass hysteria, because of course there's no such thing as a real witch. That's what historians say. However, now I'm beginning to think the historians are the ones who got it wrong," he added, an eyebrow arching expressively.

"Is it still illegal to be a witch here?" Sie asked, leaning forward and lowering her voice.

Raahi shrugged. "I don't think so. Not officially, anyway. But—"

"But what?" Sie demanded.

"Well, if they found out someone could really do magic, *real* magic, I think the government would be very, very interested."

"Why?"

"Because it would be a new kind of power, and the government doesn't want uncontrolled sources of power running around, do they?"

"Oh." Sie thought. "Could the CIA be interested in the side-door world?"

"I think they'd kill to get their hands on it," Raahi said. "Oh, sorry. I shouldn't have put it quite that way."

Sie pushed her shake away and frowned at the thought that gentle old Aunt Generous could be someone the CIA would torture or kill for information. "We've just got to rescue her," she said. "And quickly. Finish your shake."

"We shouldn't hurry. We're on a stakeout, right?"

"I'm not hungry and I didn't see steak on the menu."

"Not that kind." He smiled. "It means we're watching without being seen. Something I'm very good at. Actually, not really. That was a joke." He smiled again, hoping to cheer her up.

Sie leaned to the side to get a clearer view out the window. "Here comes that black car. It's pulling up to the curb."

"I think there's one coming from the other direction too," Raahi said, "which is odd because Newbury is one way. Listen to all that honking. They're making the other drivers awfully mad."

He was right. Another black SUV wove toward them through oncoming traffic, a blue flashing light affixed to its roof, and pulled up at an angle in front of number 234, its bumper nearly touching the first SUV. Doors opened. Men got out. Six in all. They looked pretty much the same: Light complexions, wide shoulders, straight brown hair clipped short, and black sunglasses that hid their eyes.

They swarmed up the brick walk toward the entry to 234, and one of them bent down and picked up the phone. But they did not leave once they'd found it. Instead, they listened intently (Raahi explained to Sie that they probably had little radios tucked into their ears), then they fanned out and began to search the neighboring buildings.

One of them headed for the Shake Shack.

Sie grabbed Raahi's hand and said, "Come on!"

They rushed past the waiters and behind-counter staff (also, by coincidence, all dressed in black) and pressed through the kitchen and into a storage room. "There has to be a back door!" Sie exclaimed.

"Look for a red EXIT sign," Raahi suggested. "Modern fire codes require it. It's too dark for me in here," he added apologetically, "or I would find it for you."

"Yes! Behind that stack of boxes," Sie announced. The boxes, fortunately, seemed to be empty.

She pushed them aside and was about to press the wide bar covering the door when Raahi said, "Is it alarmed?"

"I have no idea," Sie said.

"It probably is. Can you, um, make it quiet?"

"A muffling spell?" Sie asked. "Of course. Why?"

"Cast it now."

"Weave it?"

"Weave it. Whatever you do. *Before* you open the door."

She shook her head and muttered in annoyance, but then she raised her hands and spoke into the silent air around them, weaving it into a barrier that would not allow sound waves through. Her weavings, while still student level, were quite strong. She had gotten high marks for them and even been asked to demonstrate for the younger girls.

"Is it done?" Raahi asked, but he could not hear his own question. The words seemed to be sucked away and muffled by the heavy air around them. Smiling, he raised both hands and pushed hard on the bar across the metal door.

Daylight met them. They had emerged on a narrow alley with big metal dumpsters and, here and there, cars parked next to the back doors of the stores of Newbury and Boylston Streets (because the alley ran between them). The buildings pressed in on both sides, and on the alley pavement someone had painted in large lettering: Public Alley 441.

"Where now?" Raahi asked.

"This is your world, not mine," Sie hissed. "Don't you—wait, Auntie's note!" She grabbed Raahi by the wrist and turned right, pulling him around a parked car and up to the rear of another building. They stopped in front of a plain black door with bars on the small window in it. There were windows on either side, but they were barred too.

"I shouldn't do this," Sie said, frowning.

"Do what?" Raahi asked.

"This!" She gestured with both arms, her hands tracing half circles in front of her as if she were throwing open imaginary doors. A few muttered words of power (in ancient Greek, Raahi thought, but wasn't quite sure), and the door rattled and swung inward. She pulled him through it just as the sound-weaving wore off and the ringing of an alarm bell sounded from the previous building's rear door.

CHAPTER 13

Pursued

They were in a basement hallway, dimly lit, with tall, narrow wooden crates against the walls. *Must be for shipping paintings,* Sie thought. *Which means this is the right place.* She pulled Raahi ahead, guiding him around the crates, some made of fresh new plywood, others of rough old planks. "There's got to be a staircase," she said with a frown.

"We went past an elevator. I smelled the oil on the cables and I felt the steel door. Colder than the wall," he added. "Didn't you notice? Come on, I'll take you to it." He tugged her back to a flat metal wall and pushed a round button next to it. "Time to show you a little of *my* world's magic," he quipped as a bell rang and the doors slid open.

Sie did not like the way the floor moved up and down ever so slightly when they stepped in. "What is this?" she demanded as the doors closed.

"Shall we try the third floor?" he asked, pushing a button marked "3."

"Oh!" The closet they were in had begun to move upward. She gripped Raahi's arm again.

When the doors opened they revealed a completely different tableau: Elegantly appointed rooms flowing off in each direction with rich tan carpeting and, everywhere, paintings hung on the walls. The paintings were amazing: Landscapes, city scenes, portraits, harbors, children playing . . . all in lovely gold frames, and lit, each one to perfection, by cleverly placed little lights aimed down from above. They both stood there, staring.

The doors of the elevator began to shut.

"Acha!" Raahi threw his shoulder between the doors and they reversed, opening again with another *ding*. "Come on," he said, and they stepped out into the gallery.

"I see there are at least two young people who appreciate the works of the great American painters," a thin, middle-aged man said. He was wearing a dark suit. However, he did not have sunglasses, and his expression was benignly amused. "What brings you here? Any artist in particular?"

"Well," Sie said, "Auntie likes Mr. Benson's work, and Mr. Tarbell. And, um, Mr. Reid, he came to visit and made sketches of Auntie and me in front of a big Japanese screen we have in the drawing room with cranes flying on it, and he did a drawing of me sitting in a window too. Auntie's painter friends like doing sketches when they come. I think she used to sit for them as a model when she was younger, you see, and . . ." She trailed off uncertainly. The man's expression had turned from tolerant to disapproving.

"That's a very imaginative story," he said. "Are you here with your, with an . . . adult?"

Sie thought he had been about to say "your parents" but changed his mind. They did not look anything like brother and sister, of course: Her coffee-with-cream complexion reflected the "mysterious Lees," as Auntie like to put it (they had a wide variety of interesting and far-flung ancestors from Morocco all the way north to Denmark and Greenland). Her hair was dark brown and wavy—kinky in the humid summer months—and she imagined he had noticed that her physical appearance was a mix of African and other traits. Most people did.

In contrast, Raahi looked every inch the descendent of a noble Raj from India, especially when he drew himself up and put on such a stern expression. "I *beg* your pardon?" he challenged.

Sie repressed a smile; it appeared that the man's comment had deeply offended him. "You wouldn't by any chance be so discourteous as to question my friend's veracity, I trust?"

Sie smiled in spite of herself.

"Her, ah, truthfulness? No, of course not," the man hastened to say, his eyebrows rising above his horn-rimmed glasses. "I take it she favors painters from turn-of-the-century Boston. Allow me to suggest the front room." He gestured down the hall. "Let us know if you, ah, wish to discuss an acquisition." Then he swept past them down the hall, turned, and disappeared down a staircase.

"Phew," Raahi said. "I was afraid he would throw us—oh." The elevator motor had ground into motion; they could hear it distinctly behind the closed metal doors. "Do you suppose they'll come up here?"

Sie nodded. "Of course they will. Did you see them?"

"Not very clearly, to be honest," he said.

"They looked mean." She pulled something out from beneath her shirt and fingered it. It was on a string.

"Is that a good luck charm or something of the sort?" Raahi asked, trying to get a look at it.

"It's my key. Come on." She hurried down the corridor toward the front of the building. Rooms opened along the way, revealing more paintings and the occasional elegant old couch. A fresh vase of summer flowers was on a table at the end of the hall beneath an impressionistic painting of a vase full of flowers on a table in a hall. Sie passed it by and entered a large front room hung nearly floor to ceiling with paintings. "These are like the ones Auntie has," she announced.

"More coincidences," Raahi said. "You're fingering your key because you're thinking about the part in the note where it says that Mr. Vose has his own side door?"

"Yes." She approached a paneled section of wall. It was painted a dark blue-gray. It stood out from the surrounding walls, which were paneled only to chair-rail level and had linen wallpaper above. But in this one spot, the wood reached all the way to the ceiling.

Sie reached up. "Help me get this painting down."

"'Edmund Tarbell, study for *Arrangement in Pink and Gray*, this being a color sketch of G. L. pouring out the tea. The final painting hangs in the Worcester Art Museum.'" Raahi sounded very authoritative as he read the printed label on the wall beside the midsized painting of a woman in a pale summer-pink gown on a couch in front of a tea tray, a fine gray and silver Oriental screen behind her. Her brown hair fell in waves over her shoulders and she was smiling at the artist, who had worked in quick, bold strokes, as if eager to finish the sketch and sit down to tea with her.

"Why this one? There's lots of paintings," Raahi pointed out.

"G.L. stands for Generous Lee," Sie announced. "Grab the frame from the other side."

They lifted it off its hook and set it against a wall. The wood beneath the painting was smooth and undisturbed except in one small spot, at about waist height, where a dull brass keyhole was set into it.

Sie approached it nervously with her key held out. "I hope . . ." she began, then froze as raised voices echoed down the hall.

"Excuse me, gentlemen, but you may *not* tromp all through this gallery for no apparent reason!" came the voice of the man who had spoken to them.

"Out of the way," a gruff voice answered. "Now."

"I demand to see your credentials," the man from the gallery said, his voice rising.

"How's this for a credential," another voice barked.

"A gun? Put that away at once! We have priceless art in here! I insist you—*hey!*"

It sounded like they had pushed past him. Heavy footsteps thudded in the hall.

"Quick!" Raahi cried.

Silent pressed the key into the keyhole. It fit. She turned it.

There was a click, and a doorframe rose out of the wooden wall. It was painted the same blue-gray as the wall and so was the door within the frame. There was a tarnished brass knob just above the keyhole. Sie turned the knob. The door swung open.

They hurried through into another room full of paintings, and Sie pushed the door closed behind them.

"Turn the key again," Raahi said, "so the door disappears."

"Right." She slipped her key into the keyhole, which (like most old locks) went straight through the door and could take a key from either side. She turned the key. There was another click and the door faded into a similar wall of wooden paneling.

"Good afternoon," a man's deep voice said from behind them. "What brings you here?"

"Oh! Thank goodness!" Sie exclaimed. "It's Mr. Vose! Uh, do you remember me? My great aunt used to come here sometimes, but she's been—"

"My dear girl," he cut in, still sounding friendly. He was an older man in a comfortable brown suit with a mustache and eyes that blinked out from behind gold-rimmed glasses. "Of course I recall you. Tea at your aunt's, why, it must have been several years ago. How you've grown!" He guided them down the hall, the same hall they'd just been in except there were people in old-fashioned clothing studying various paintings. "Come to my office, won't you?"

They turned into a side room with a large desk covered in papers. The walls were hung with paintings, dozens and dozens of them, so thickly that you could not really tell what the wallpaper pattern was.

He gestured to an old-fashioned couch beneath a wide landscape of a port, the docks crowded with tall-masted ships. "Make yourselves comfortable." He looked out the door, then closed it and turned the lock. "What brings you here, Silent?"

"You *do* remember me," Sie said, looking pleased.

"Oh yes. You realize that it's a rare thing to be entrusted with a key?" His eyes traveled from Sie over to Raahi, then back to her. "And that the keyholder is expected to maintain The Confidence?" (Of course he wasn't writing down what he said, but they could tell from his emphasis that both The and Confidence ought to be capitalized.)

"I'm sorry I used it in front of him," Sie said. "But they were about to catch us and I couldn't think of anything else to do."

"And *they* would be . . .?"

"The CIA. I think they've got Aunt Gen."

"What does that stand for?" he asked.

"Generous," Raahi offered.

"No, CIA," he said with a frown, focusing on Sie not Raahi.

"I forget," Sie admitted. "Spies of some kind."

"If I may?" Raahi asked.

They stared at him.

"The Central Intelligence Agency was formed in 1941. Prior to that, spies were run by the War Department's Military Intelligence Division."

"I've heard of that, all right. We call it G-2," Mr. Vose said. He frowned. "At this juncture, we're cooperative. Are you telling me that in your world, the intelligence services are our *enemy?*"

"Those men didn't seem at *all* friendly," Sie said.

"That's unfortunate. The desire for power is a dangerous thing, isn't it?"

Sie and Raahi exchanged a puzzled glance.

"Speaking of power," Mr. Vose continued, "It seems that the Lees have a universal key. Most of the keys open only a specific door."

"Oh. I didn't even think. I just tried it on your door and it worked," Sie explained.

"How did you know about my door?" Mr. Vose asked, his eyes narrowed.

"A note from my aunt."

He relaxed. "I see. Is *her* passage properly protected?"

"Her door?" Raahi asked.

"Precisely. Is it still, ah, operating normally?"

Sie shrugged. "We don't know," she explained. "My mother's selling the house."

"Selling? But that's strictly forbidden! I'm not familiar with your mother. Is she a Lee?"

Sie nodded. "But I'm afraid she's . . ." She shrugged rather helplessly.

"Are you *sure* she's a Lee?" he asked, eyeing her narrowly.

"Well, I guess so. She doesn't, um, have any talent for, you know—"

"Magic? Interesting. But perhaps a talent for deception?" He was still eyeing her in a way that made her think he knew something. "Do you take after her?"

"Um, not really. Auntie says I'm the spitting image of her. Auntie, I mean. When she was young. And I look like her old pictures. We don't seem to have any pictures of my mother when she was young."

"Interesting. Well, the key concern, if you'll pardon the expression, is to stop that woman from selling the house. As the keyholder, you're responsible for that door. Don't lose control of it." Mr. Vose looked quite stern. "Do you understand?"

Sie shrugged. "I don't see what *I* can do. I'm a minor. I have no legal standing. Can't you come through and help us?"

Mr. Vose reached into the top drawer of his desk and extracted a brass key of antique design. "I have not been through my door for several years," he said, studying the key as he turned it over in his hands. "I fear I will never use it again."

"Are you saying you can't help?" Raahi asked.

"I'm saying . . ." He paused, fingering the key, then he let it drop back in the drawer.

When he did not continue, Sie leaned forward and said, "Does it make you ill? That's what happened to Auntie. After a while, she couldn't anymore. She used to always go there, well, *here*, to shop and visit friends, and when I was younger she'd walk me to and from school. She wore the key then, like I do now. But she said it was making her sick."

He sighed deeply. "Sometimes it wears on us. At first I was quite active in the work of the SDC, the, ah, Side Door Council. But after other-world sorcerers breached the door at the old Tremont Temple and we had to push them back, not to mention the fire that had to be extinguished afterward, I was ill for several months. I haven't been able to cross over since, and nowadays I can't even do the simplest working. I'm sorry, Silent. I do hope you find your aunt. She was—is—a wonderful person." He stood. "By now I imagine the search for you has moved on and you can go back through. I'll keep the door ajar until you confirm that it's safe."

"You're sending us back?" Sie demanded, rising to her feet. "I thought you'd help."

"He has," Raahi said. "We weren't caught, right?"

Mr. Vose frowned. "I wish I could be more helpful, but I'm all used up from past battles, I'm afraid. I'm dreadfully sorry, my dear." He had come around his desk, and now he leaned over and patted Sie on the head, a gesture which she did not appreciate. "But now you know where my door is, and if the need arises, do come through again. I'll hide you as best I can."

"Thank you, Mr. Vose." Raahi bowed politely. "I gather from the bell of your mantle clock that it is now a quarter past five. Is the gallery closed?"

He nodded.

"Let's see if the other Vose Gallery is as quiet as this one," Raahi said.

"Wait," Sie said. "He needs to tell us if there's anyone else." She paused in the hall.

"Anyone else?" Mr. Vose repeated. "I don't understand."

"Does anyone have a key." Sie frowned. "Does anyone know about weavings and workings? Isn't there *anyone* in the modern world who could help?"

"Ah." Mr. Vose nodded. "There may be, as a matter of fact."

"Do you have a name?" Sie demanded.

"Well, a title, at least. You could look for the Custodian. There's supposed to be one in each world."

"*Each* world?" Sie repeated. "How many worlds are there?"

Mr. Vose shrugged. "I can tell you that each world has a close match. Worlds come in pairs, usually one having much more magic than the other. And I believe that three pairs make up a set. In your modern world, scientists have measured a lot of invisible mass—they call it black matter—but that's really just the parallel worlds of our set, isn't it?"

Raahi gaped at him. "Is it?" he demanded.

"I believe so, but I'm no expert. And I have *no* idea how many sets there might be beyond our own. My point is, the Custodians are in charge of keeping them all in order, which means, mostly, not letting people mess around with boundaries. It's a very important position and he or she might not take an interest in your case, but you can certainly ask. Good luck!" He pushed them gently toward the door.

"How do we find her?" Sie asked.

"*She* usually finds *you*, but you could ask at the library. Now you really *must* be on your way. The staff will be coming around soon to do the inventory, and it would be difficult to explain your presence to them."

"I don't understand," Raahi said. "Your name is on this establishment. Can't you just tell them to wait?"

Mr. Vose looked sad. "Young man," he said, "my health has deteriorated to such an extent that I recently had to turn management over to an interim director. At present, he's in charge and I'm still officially on sick leave. It was just good luck that I was here today. I came in because we were opening a new exhibition."

"I see," Raahi said. "Sorry about that. I hope you feel better soon, sir."

"Thank you. Now please be careful and don't underestimate your enemies. There are always people who want to use the doors to further their own agendas, if you know what I mean."

"I'm not sure I do," Sie said, pausing with the key held out. "What agendas?"

Mr. Vose leaned toward them and replied in a whisper. "Imagine what would happen if someone came here from your side with modern weapons and a crack force of ruthless men, perhaps in dark suits, determined to find a key and use it for nefarious purposes?"

"Those men *are* after my key," Sie said.

"Not just the key. The door, too," Raahi added. "And now that your mother has control of your aunt's house, they can use it whenever they want. Or," he frowned in thought, "remove it from the house and take it to, well, wherever they wanted. Then they could try to steal magic and bring it back."

Mr. Vose nodded grimly. "Precisely the kind of abuse we need to prevent. *You* need to prevent."

Sie frowned. "If I can find Aunt Gen, then…" Sie bit her lip. "Hopefully she'll know what to do." She pulled out her key, fitted it into the keyhole, and the door appeared. Her hand on the knob, she turned and asked, "Which public library?"

"The new one on Copley Square," Mr. Vose said. "Well, new to me. They had to destroy the old building on Boylston in 1899 when the previous Custodian was attacked by a rogue band of wizards who wanted to take over your world. The only way to stop them was to blow up the entire building. I'm sure you're familiar with as important an historical event as that one?"

"It was replaced with an office building and a theater," Raahi said. "But I never heard anything about a battle. Speaking of history, I thought your gallery was on Copley Square in the early 1900s, but here we are still on Newbury Street."

"Maybe in your world. But in your world, the gallery doesn't have a side door."

"We went through the side door!" Raahi objected.

"In *your* history it doesn't. You're in my present now. Different, of course."

"Of course." But Raahi's expression was still doubtful.

Sie glanced between them. "History's told differently on your side of the door, Raahi. Come on, let's go."

"Or else he's off his rocker," Raahi muttered as they stepped into the newer gallery and the door clicked closed behind them.

The lights were out and the building was quiet. It seemed the modern Vose Gallery was also closed. They rehung the painting of Aunt Gen, then hurried down the carpeted corridor past the vase of flowers and toward the stairs.

Raahi caught Sie's arm at the top of the stairs and hissed, "Red light, flashing, up there." He pointed toward a little device mounted on the staircase wall.

"What is it?" Sie asked.

"Probably a motion detector. It's their security system. Of course they'd switch it on when the gallery's closed."

"Is that bad?" Sie asked.

"It'll bring the police, and those men might listen to the police radio frequencies. Can you do something?"

"I don't even know how these things work," she said, staring at the strange little device.

"It runs on electricity. A sudden charge might short it out. Break it," he added when she looked puzzled. "I don't suppose you can make lightning?" He looked at her hopefully.

"We aren't supposed to mess with weather. Very disruptive. They only do that at the Central Resources for Agricultural Planning office, I think." She frowned.

"Would that be abbreviated as CRAP? Raahi asked.

"Yes. I think it's to remind us of how much trouble you can get into when you try to adjust the weath—uh oh!" Sie had been interrupted by an alarm bell sounding from somewhere downstairs. "Well, I suppose just this once. Stand back." She raised both hands. She chanted something that made Raahi's hair stand up. She began to turn slowly, then faster, her arms raised and her eyes closed. (He wondered why she didn't get dizzy and fall over.) Then she finished with another strange chant and clapped her hands.

The clap did not stop. It seemed to be picked up and to roll around the sky above the building. The rumbles grew into a series of tremendous thunder claps that shook the building. A sizzling, a bright flash and a puff of smoke from the little device on the staircase told them it had been disabled.

Rain sluiced down the window at the end of the hall. The alarm bell stopped. "How's that?" Sie asked.

Raahi stared at her. "Did you really just . . ." He gestured toward the flashes of lighting and heavy rain outside the nearest window.

"Well, you asked me to. Come on." And then she hurried down the staircase, leaving Raahi to feel his way down after her.

He was just emerging on the first floor when he heard a loud "Crack!" from the front of the building. "And that must be the front door," he said to himself with a grin as he hurried to catch up with her.

CHAPTER 14

Forced to Retreat

They came down the wide steps in front of the gallery and paused on the wet sidewalk. The rain had stopped as quickly as it started, and it was becoming a pleasant summer evening. Many of the businesses were open and bustling with activity. The sidewalk was busy and so was the road, but the three long, black SUVs parked a little way up the street caught their attention at once. And then Sie noticed that there were men, at least two, maybe three, lurking back in the shadows at the entry to 234—the building where they thought Aunt Gen might be.

"We can't go there. Not now," she said. "We can't even walk past it. They'll see us for sure. Come on." She tugged Raahi out into a crowd of shoppers and, keeping in the middle of them, headed the other way down Newbury. At the Gloucester Street light, with a long block between them and the SUVs, she thought it would be safe to cross the street. The next block was where Aunt Gen's brick house stood, its bow windows dark and empty. Sie hurried them up to it, then paused on the sidewalk. "Darn!" she said, fingering the key.

"Aren't we going into your aunt's house?" Raahi asked.

"I wanted to go in by the side door, but we didn't go out that way."

"What's the difference?" Raahi asked.

"Notice any side doors?"

"Oh!" The building was hemmed in on one side by a similar brick house. On the other, a narrow alley ran beside it. The alley was fenced off and paved, and the wall of the house was covered with ivy and had neither door nor windows in it.

"When I go out the side door, that alley is part of our garden and there isn't that big building shadowing it. Things are different."

"We can always go in the front door," Raahi pointed out. "Are you looking for something?"

"I'm looking for a place to stay," Sie said. "And more clues. I want to look through Auntie's desk and see if there are any other names I can try. Maybe one of her friends will be more helpful than Mr. Vose was. Also, assuming we can get in, I could use my side door key to go back again. I was thinking about going to my old school in the morning to ask my teachers for help. And I can't go back to the cousins' house, can I?"

"I could ask my mother if—"

"No, I'll be fine. She must be expecting you for dinner. I'll walk you home."

Raahi looked insulted. "*I'm* the one who's looking after *you*," he insisted. "I assure you I can find my way around Back Bay."

Sie smiled. "Thanks for helping me today," she said. "I really appreciate it. And I know you're better than me at getting around, at least in this world. But they *saw* you. In fact, they took your picture. I'm sorry I put you at risk, Raahi, but we have to face facts. It may not be safe for you to walk around here anymore. Especially alone."

He paused, frowning. "Do you have any hats?"

"Why?" Sie stared at him.

"I'll need a disguise," he said. "Maybe a fedora or something else with a brim?"

Sie laughed. She didn't mean to, but she couldn't help it. Maybe she needed to let off tension after the strange and frightening events of the day. Anyway, she laughed for quite a long time.

"I'm feeling a bit insulted," Raahi complained.

"I'm sorry," she said. "I'm not making fun of you! It's just, I guess I'm a little hysterical. And, um, I don't think a hat would do enough to disguise you from those spies. But feel free to look through the hall closet for one. Come on." And then she lead him up the steps to the front door. Of course it was locked, but she recalled that there was a tarnished old key in the big terra-cotta urn that held a box-wood plant. She stuck her fingers in the dry, crumbly soil and felt around. All around. The key was not there. "Darn! Mother must've taken it."

"Can't you . . . ?" Raahi asked.

Sie frowned. "Is anyone watching?"

Raahi turned and studied the sidewalk. "I don't think so."

"We should be certain."

"When you can't see very well, you do develop your sense of when someone's eyes are on you. And I don't sense that anyone's watching us now."

"All right. But this is tricky because I don't want to break the lock." She frowned and placed her hand over the keyhole. Closing her eyes, she muttered a gentle opening request, weaving it first into the stale, hot air of the keyhole, then beginning, carefully, to weave it into the metal of the tumblers of the lock.

The leaves of the trees shading the sidewalk rustled oddly for a moment.

The lock clicked.

Sie opened her eyes and tried the handle, and the door sprang open. It was a heavy oak door with a round glass window in it.

"Nice work!" Raahi exclaimed.

Boxes were stacked in the front hall, taped and addressed, they soon discovered, to "Colonial Farm Road, McLean, Virginia." Sie wondered why her mother would send all Auntie's belongings to a farm. She gave one of the boxes a little shake. It rattled. "What's Mother up to?" she asked with a frown.

Raahi flipped on the electric light switch and leaned over to study one of the labels. "It's not a farm," he said. "It's where the CIA is based. Why would she send everything to the Central Intelligence Agency?"

"No idea," Sie said. "Is *everything* packed?" She went through the hall and into the parlor, then into the little library behind it, where most of the books had been taken down from the shelves and stacked on the floor as if on the way to being put into boxes. She went back into the hall and through the dining room, where the mantle and sideboard were bare and the chandelier had been taken down and left on the dining table. Then she went into the kitchen, *their* cozy kitchen, where the cabinets were open and an unfamiliar big plastic trash can was overflowing with all their familiar boxes and tins from the pantry. "She's throwing our food away!" Sie objected, stopping to stare unhappily at the sight.

"Where is your, ah, side door?" Raahi asked.

"Behind that big piece of plywood nailed up in the parlor," Sie said. "The one that says in orange spray paint, 'Remove for trans-port'."

"Oh dear," Raahi said.

They stood in silence for a moment, each lost in thought, until Raahi stirred and said, "One thing's for sure. You obviously can't stay here. Someone will come back to finish the packing. Probably bright and early tomorrow morning, don't you think?"

Sie turned to say something in reply, but suddenly the enormity of the situation overcame her: Her only real family, dear Aunt Gen, gone and probably a captive of those horrible men; the cousins away and renting their house to some nasty strangers; and now the home she had grown up in on the verge of being taken from her forever. She started to cry. She *never* cried, but for some reason, she could not stop herself.

Sobbing, she rushed from the kitchen and ran up the stairs to her cozy little bedroom. Pushing the door open, she was brought to a sudden and complete stop. She had been following an instinctive urge to throw herself down on her bed, *but there was no bed*. The headboard and footboard were leaning against the wall, along with some long boards that must have formed the sides. The mattress was propped up against another wall. And that was all. The rest of her furniture and belongings—her clothing, her childhood dolls, all her precious and wonderful books, even her cello—they were simply and horribly *not there*. She stood staring at the empty floorboards and bare walls. Then she turned and, too shocked and saddened even to cry again, stumbled back down the stairs to where Raahi was standing in the hallway, waiting for her.

"I'm sorry," he said. "I'm really very sorry. It must be awful for you." It was all he could think to say.

She took a deep breath and straightened her spine. Her eyes flashed dangerously. "The public library," she said. "I'm going. Now! Uh, want to go with me?"

"Absolutely! I'm with you all the way, Miss Lee." He smiled. And, in spite of herself, Sie smiled back. It did at least feel good to have a friend to share her misadventures with, even a friend as strange and unexpected as Raahi.

CHAPTER 15

Attacked

They went down to the end of the block and turned left on Hereford to make sure the men did not see them. Then they turned right on Boylston at the next block and made their way along the busy sidewalk toward downtown. It was only four blocks to the library, a huge old building with arches in front of it that occupied the entire area between Exeter and Dartmouth Streets. As they neared it, Sie said, "Do you want to call your mother?"

Raahi shrugged. "Not so easy. I don't have a cell phone and they've taken most of the pay phones away. Can we send her a note by bird?"

"I don't usually do things like that," Sie said.

"How about in the *other* world?" Raahi asked.

"No, not even there. We study workings and weavings and influences in school, but we aren't supposed to actually *use* them. And most students can't really do that much." She shrugged.

"Why not?" Raahi pressed. "I thought it was a school for magic."

"They teach us theory and history in our lectures. The labs are where we get to practice, and trust me, most people need a *lot* of practice."

"Oh! So you're a natural, then?" he asked. "I *thought* you seemed unusually talented." He smiled.

"I don't know," Sie said with a frown. "Some things seem to come easily to me. Maybe because Auntie was . . ."

"Was what? Wait, are there certain people in the other world who do magic and others who don't? Like witches, right?"

"Auntie used to do workings and weavings for people. That's how she made her living when she was younger. She had a talent for it."

"And you have talent too. But not your mother?"

Sie shrugged. "None that I know of. Maybe she's envious."

"Or worse. She knows about the other world, right?'

"Yes. And she must've told those men from the CIA."

"The ones who drive against traffic?" Raahi asked, looking worried.

"Yes, but—wait, the honking?" She stopped.

"Afraid so. Sounds like they're coming up Dartmouth Street the wrong way to head us off at the library. I can't imagine how much trouble they're causing. They probably came up Newbury the wrong way too."

"Down Exeter, quick!" Sie cried, tugging Raahi to the right and hurrying alongside a tall, modern cement structure.

"This is the new part of the library," Raahi said.

"Really? It looks awful! I doubt a Custodian would be in there. Let's go to the rear of the old building. Hurry." They swung around the modern structure, turning left where a street sign said "Blagden" and rushing along the empty sidewalk. Halfway up the block, the modern cement gave way to old-fashioned stone with high windows and, in the middle, a black-painted double door, firmly locked and marked "Emergency Exit Only." Sie stopped in front of it and made her opening gesture in the air.

The door creaked slowly outward, and a red light above it began to blink.

"Bravo," Raahi said. "You're getting quite good at breaking and entering." He grinned again.

"Come," she said, her expression grim as she tugged him into the dimly lit interior and the doors swung closed behind them.

It was not the library she remembered with its vaulting ceilings, brightly painted murals, and wide, airy stairs all done in rich, golden-yellow Italian marble. It was instead a rather ordinary work area with narrow halls and offices on both sides. "Friends of the Library," one door announced. A window set in the door offered a view of rows of desks, deserted by that hour, and in the distance, a larger window that offered a glimpse of green.

"The courtyard," Sie exclaimed, pleased to see something she recognized. "Come on." She gestured and muttered and the door sprang open, its glass window cracking from the force of the working.

They ran past desks and chairs and came to a big window with its view of a huge interior courtyard, planted elegantly, and with a pool of water in its middle. "There weren't so many offices in *my* library," Sie complained. "It was much more open."

"Modern progress," Raahi said. "Not always a good thing. How do we find the Custodian?"

"No idea, but we better hurry. Too bad this window has iron bars." She pressed a hand against the cold glass. "I'd like to get into the courtyard," she said. "From there we could enter the main library and explore the reading rooms. Do you mind?"

"Mind what?" Raahi asked.

She shrugged. "This might be a little more destructive than what I've done before."

He backed away from the window as Sie raised her hands and began to chant.

The glass and iron gave way all at once, bursting in a spray of thousands of sparkling bits of glass scattering explosively out into the courtyard along with bright red sparks of molten iron. People who had been enjoying the tranquility of the courtyard turned to stare, their faces registering shock and alarm.

"I didn't know it would make so much noise," Sie complained.

"It sure did," Raahi said. "Uh, we better climb through before the fire department and police come. I'm sure people are calling 911 on their cell phones."

"Extension nine hundred and eleven?" Sie asked, puzzled. "What's that?" (Her Aunt Gen rarely used their antique telephone and since her classmates were in a different world, she never had reason to.)

"I'll explain later. Let's just go."

They brushed aside broken chunks of glass on the windowsill and climbed up and over, landing with crunching sounds on more broken glass and bits of cooling iron. People had flooded into the courtyard to stare and point and exchange startled exclamations.

"Must have been a gas leak, but we're okay," Raahi said as they pressed into the crowd. As soon as they had pushed through the eager gawkers, Sie hurried them toward the front entrance of the library. Soon they were standing in the lobby at the base of the huge stairs, looking up toward grand vaulting walls and ceilings with elaborate old paintings of mythical scenes. Outside, loud honking and the squealing of brakes told a more modern story of square-jawed, mirthless men rushing toward them in black SUVs.

"We need to move," Raahi said. "Up?"

They began to climb the stairs.

"Hold it!" Someone with a deep, commanding voice and a mean-looking black gun was standing behind them at the bottom of the staircase, and more men in dark suits were running across the lobby. Soon there was a crowd of men with guns at the bottom of the stairs, glaring up at Sie and Raahi.

And then Sie's mother came through the swinging glass doors and across the lobby, her expensive black pumps making a *tap tap tap* sound on the marble floor.

She walked up to the front row of men and stopped beside the one who had spoken to them. "Ah, Silent," she said. "I would rather not have to harm you. Just give us the key and we'll let you go home."

"I don't have a home, thanks to you," Sie snapped. "And for your information, you're never going to get my key!"

The lead man leaned toward Sie's mother and asked in a whisper that unfortunately carried up the staircase clearly enough for Sie and Raahi to hear, "Should I shoot her?"

"Not quite yet," her mother said. "I believe all children should be allowed second chances. Except," she added, "that one." She pointed at Raahi. "Shoot him now to show her we mean business."

CHAPTER 16

Defensive Maneuvers

Raahi's face fell and he gripped Sie's arm so tightly she let out an involuntary "Ow!"

Then she closed her eyes and visualized the first thing she could think of, which might not have been the wisest thing, she realized a moment later, as the glass doors shattered inward and a dozen wild-eyed wolves came racing and growling and howling into the lobby, leaping at the men in black suits and gripping their pants and legs and jackets and arms in slobbering, angry, sharp-toothed jaws. In a moment it was complete and utter mayhem, with men shouting and shooting and wolves howling and growling all over the shiny marble floor.

People who had been hiding in the rooms to either side of the lobby ran away screaming or darted bravely around the angry tangle of men and wolves to race out the broken doors onto Boylston Street. Sirens began to sound from outside, drawing nearer.

In the confusion, Sie tugged Raahi's hand and drew him up the stairs to a landing then around a corner and up more stairs to the wide second floor. There they stopped, panting, to take their bearings.

"A rather clever illusion," someone said. "But it won't stop them for long. Have you given any thought to more permanent solutions?"

They spun around to find themselves facing a small man in a wrinkled khaki suit and gold-rimmed glasses. His skin was weathered and dark, his black-going-gray hair was cut short, and there were numerous fine wrinkle lines at the corners of his eyes, suggesting he smiled often. He was smiling at them now.

"We have to find the Custodian," Sie said, sounding breathless. "There's been a terrible, I mean, all sorts of terrible things have happened, and, and I have to rescue—"

"Please." He held up a hand. "Let's focus our attention on what to do *now*, not on what has already gone wrong. Regrets never solved a problem." He smiled warmly, as if expecting them to appreciate the cleverness of his comment.

Raahi took a turn. "Do you know where we can find her, sir? It's really *very* urgent. Already there has been some damage done to this lovely library," he added. It seemed likely that the man worked there. He had a comfortable way of standing, with one hand tucked into a pocket and the other pressing an old leather-bound volume to his side.

"It's always urgent, young man. If you are going to make a career out of this sort of thing, you had best accept that. Now, what do you think, Silent? Can you resolve this fully and finally?"

"Fully and finally?" She stared at him. "Do you know the instructors at my school? Because that's how they talk about a weaving that makes a full circle and completes itself. Right?"

He nodded. "Very good! And that is the only kind of weaving that changes things so completely that no one but the weaver and his or her collaborators can recall the way it was before. The so-called complete shift, yes?"

"I thought that was just theoretical. Wait, how do you know my name? Can we even trust you?"

He smiled again and walked toward them. "Of course you must ask such questions. You are doing very well. I'm pleased. Your headmistress was right about you, and so was Generous. When she gave you the key, she gambled on your growing into the position.

Trial by fire, you might say. I was opposed, but it was her decision to make, not mine. Custodians do not tell people what to do; we simply watch over things, as it were. Now, here, if I'm not mistaken, come those over-enthusiastic government agents, lead by your purported mother, who is, I'm afraid, not one of your greatest assets. It's a shame she ever learned about your aunt's side door, isn't it? Otherwise, she might still be safely out of town in search of other 'exotic spices,' as she likes to put it."

"Wait, are you suggesting I should reweave the entire story?"

"You may reweave only your *own* story, Silent, but your adoptive mother weaves in and out of your story on occasion, doesn't she? Seek the moment where your story and hers met and the seeds of the current problem were planted. Then reweave that event the way you think it ought to be."

"Adoptive? What . . . ? Uh, never mind about that now," she added hurriedly as shouting came from the staircase. "They teach us that weaving real stories isn't permitted. It's reweaving reality, isn't it?" Sie asked. "We aren't supposed to do that. Ever."

"Not at school, certainly." He grinned again. "If you fail to get an A, you must just live with the fact, rather than reweave your exam. Students have been thrown out of magical worlds for less. Not to mention being thrown out of school, of course. But sometimes, a bit of judicious reweaving is necessary." He turned and gestured toward the top of the stairs, where running men, guns drawn, were sprinting into view.

"Oh no!" Sie exclaimed. "I don't know if I—"

But Raahi whispered, "You can do it!" at the same moment that a gun popped loudly and the nasty whiz of a bullet came toward them down the long marble hall.

Sie closed her eyes and drew herself up tall and still. Her lips moved rapidly in a silent chant. Her hair began to rise as if full of electricity. Raahi, standing beside her, felt his hair begin to rise too.

Inside her trance, Sie was flipping back through events, going back to where the first thing went wrong. She paused on the chilly day when Aunt Gen had gotten a cold and taken to her bed, giving Mother an excuse to take Sie away for the weekend—and never bring her back. But it had started long before then, hadn't it?

She was in the parlor with Auntie one Christmas many years ago, opening gifts and laughing in a little girl laugh that she hardly recognized as her own, when her mother had, to their surprise, knocked on the front door and entered, gray overcoat buttoned and a black hat pulled low.

"I've come for the holiday," she announced. "And to see how the child is doing in school."

Aunt Gen had frowned. "She's doing fine. I send you reports by mail. As far as I can tell, you never bother to read them."

"I'd like to see her school and speak to her teachers," her mother had said. "If you don't mind?"

Aunt Gen had not looked happy, but she had shrugged and said, "I suppose I could have her teacher come over some evening to talk with you."

"She is legally *my* daughter," her mother had said. "And I can take her away from you if I want to!"

"Please don't," Sie had said in a small voice, clinging to Auntie's arm.

"Then show me how to get to your school," her mother had hissed, taking a threatening step forward.

"Now, now, of course the school is closed over the holidays," Aunt Gen had said. "But if you'll come back in a week or two . . ."

"Silent! How do you get to school?" her mother had demanded, looming above her.

"With Auntie's key," she'd blurted out. "Through the side door. There." She'd pointed to the little doorway that was set into a frame on the wall of the library.

"Don't be silly! It's obviously just decorative," her mother had snapped. "Since there's no corresponding door on the outside. Unless . . ." She seemed to be struck by a thought.

"It is best you don't know about that," Aunt Gen had said, her tone stern. "Not in your line of work. I'm sorry, but I cannot show you. Don't bother Silent about it, either. I won't stand for it."

"On the contrary, it is vital that I know about such things, given my line of work." Her mother was eyeing the door in a calculating manner. "Silent, bring me that key. Now."

Sie, feeling very small and bullied, had done what her mother ordered and opened the door. Then her mother had stood there, staring out onto the side-door world for a long time before she turned and, eyes blazing with excitement, said, "You've been keeping this from me, haven't you, Gen? I shall come back soon and make you tell me *all* about it!"

Then a taxi driver had honked to remind her that he was waiting, and off her mother had gone again, to who knows where. Apparently she had never intended to "stay for the holidays" after all.

But now the older Sie was watching the scene from her trance and before her younger self could give the secret away, she decided to step in and reweave. So she slipped right into the Christmas morning scene in place of her younger self and stood up, facing her mother, eyes flashing dangerously.

Aunt Gen gasped, and her mother took a frightened step backward. "Who are *you?*" she demanded. "And how did you get here?"

"In the future," Sie said, eyeing her mother narrowly, "you will try to take the Lee Family's key. I will be older, like this, and the keeper of it."

"Good heavens," Aunt Gen said. "It's you, Sie! Are you reweaving?"

"Yes. It must be done. Mother, *you will not recall this day*. Nor will you remember that we have a key. You will believe that I went— go—to an ordinary school called, um . . . (and then she remembered that she *was* going to an ordinary school that would do perfectly for the weaving) . . . the Quincy School. I'm an ordinary student, mostly Bs, and I show no aptitude for magic. You will put any thoughts of using other worlds or the doors between them out of your mind and not promote your own career by pursuing powers that you have no right to. That is all. Merry Christmas." And then she slipped back to the current moment, allowing her younger self to return to the scene.

She was standing on the second floor of the Boston Public Library with Raahi and the man in the khaki suit again. She spun around, wondering where the gunshot had come from and whether it was going to hit anyone. But the men in dark suits were gone. There were just ordinary everyday people going to and fro, books beneath their arms.

"What did you do to them?" Raahi asked.

"I rewove things so they weren't chasing us. Mother doesn't know about the side door now. Or the key."

"How? Did you erase her memory?" Raahi looked puzzled.

"She went back and changed the incident that first started her mother thinking about the key," the man said. "Well done, Sie. I slipped back behind you and observed. Not to pry but just to make sure everything went smoothly. You did very well. Most professional. Hard to believe you are only in high school."

"Not until September," she said. "Or later, if I don't figure out how to register and apply."

"Really! Well, you will have an illustrious career, I should think. Oh, and here *you* go, young man," he added, slipping a hand into his jacket pocket and producing a bullet. "I took the liberty of diverting this before I slipped back to watch Sie reweave. I'm afraid it was heading for your shoulder."

Raahi took it with raised eyebrows. "Uh, thanks," he said. "Thanks very much."

"Now, why don't you go and get your poor aunt? Although your so-called mother will no longer recall quite why she had your aunt detained, the fact remains that your aunt is still in custody. She was captured too far back in time for this reweaving to undo that event. It's been woven into multiple other stories by now."

"Oh no! We've got to get her! Come on, Raahi." And they were off at a jog, rushing downstairs and through the bookish crowd, leaving a wake of disapproving glares behind them.

CHAPTER 17

The Hornet's Nest

It was past six by then, and Raahi agreed that his mother would probably be worried. However, he was unwilling to delay the rescue mission. So they hurried out the (no longer broken) front doors and headed toward Newbury Street as fast as they could. The sidewalks were crowded, it being a pleasant summer evening, and sidewalk cafes were full to overflowing with early diners. Still, they made it to the block where the gallery was located in record time and arrived, panting, at the entry to 234.

Silent might have changed her own story by preventing her mother from learning about the side door key, but she had not altered the story of the building. It looked just the same, stern and unwelcoming, and its oak door was firmly locked. Peeking in, they could see that the brass sign next to the elevator still listed the same anonymous-sounding businesses offering short-term rental rooms.

"We've got to find out if Aunt Gen is in one of these suites," Sie said.

"How?" Raahi asked.

Sie frowned. "I don't know. Suggestions?"

"Unlock the front door then knock on each apartment and call her name?" Raahi offered.

It was a simplistic plan, but it seemed practical. "Right," Sie said, leaning over the door. But there was no keyhole and no old fashioned tumbler like at Aunt Gen's. There was instead a metal pad with numbered buttons on it. She sent her magic trickling into the cracks but could not figure out how it worked. And without an understanding of the mechanics, she could not unlock it. "Darn!" she muttered. "I'm going to have to . . ." She stepped back, raised her hands, muttered an appeal to draw wind to her, and pushed it hard at the doorway.

The door splintered off its hinges and fell onto the marble floor of the entry hall with a crash. People sitting at outdoor tables over at the Shake Shack jumped up and leaned over the railing to try to see what had happened. Sie pulled Raahi forward, stepping around the door where it lay in the middle of the floor.

"Are you *trying* to attract attention?" he complained.

"Let's just hurry," Sie said, leading the way down the hall to the first door. It was marked, in brass lettering, No. 1. She knocked repeatedly, but no one answered. "Aunt Gen?" she called. Still no answer. "I don't think she's in there," she said.

"Best to be sure," Raahi said.

Crash. The door splintered inward and Sie leaned in and scanned the interior. "I'm sure," she said. "Next one."

They tried No. 2, further down the hall. No answer there either. Another crash and another look within, but Sie shook her head. "Empty too," she said with a frown. "Let's try the second floor."

They hurried to the elevator and Raahi pushed the up button.

A small sign lit up: *Insert key card here.* There was a narrow slot beneath the sign. "We better take the stairs," Raahi said.

Upstairs, an annoyed air flight attendant answered at No. 3, complaining that she had just gotten in from Holland and would they please not disturb her. No one answered at No. 4. "Probably out to dinner," Raahi suggested.

"I don't think anyone's staying there right now," Sie said.

"How can you tell?" Raahi asked.

"I get a feeling if someplace is lived in. Different from an empty place. They feel all still and stuffy from no one opening the windows or door."

"Or running an air conditioner," Raahi said. "It's hot in this hall. No central air."

"What's central hair?" Sie asked, and Raahi tried not to laugh as Sie gestured and the door fell inward with a crash. "See? Empty," she said.

"I guess it can't be helped about the doors," Raahi said as they turned and headed for the stairs again.

Up on the third floor, they found four doors instead of two. "Smaller apartments, I guess," Raahi said. "Probably servants' rooms in the old days."

No one answered at the first two doors, so they were also unceremoniously smashed inward, revealing empty studio apartments. The third apartment had a small entry hall with another closed door leading out of it, so Sie smashed it too. "No one here," she announced as she returned to Raahi who had waited in the entry, wondering what she'd break next.

"Do you think a more stealthy approach might be prudent?" he asked, but Sie ignored him.

At the fourth apartment, an elderly man thumped to the door with the aid of a cane and said, "Stop bothering me with all that banging and smashing! I'm trying to nap." Apologizing, they turned and hurried upstairs to the fourth floor, where again there were four doors, locked and quiet. "I don't think they're occupied, but I should make sure," she said.

"Do you have to open them so violently?"

She shrugged. "It's faster, but . . ." This time, she stopped to cup her hands over the locks and mutter, so that the latches clicked and the doors swung open. Raahi was impressed by her technique, but unfortunately these rooms were empty too.

"So few guests," Raahi said. "It makes you wonder if the apartments are just a front. But for what, exactly?"

Sie frowned. "Wasn't there a fifth floor on the directory?"

"Wormwood Suites," Raahi said. "Strange name, don't you think?"

"Artemisia absinthium, a silver-leaved plant with golden flowers that is often used in potions . . . well, maybe not in *this* world. But it's used for medicines here, I think."

Raahi smiled. "Now you're sounding like me. It's used in drinks too."

"What, like soda pops?"

"Sodas? No. Alcoholic beverages. Old-fashioned ones. Absinthe, for instance."

"Which is?" Sie asked.

Raahi shrugged. "No idea, really. It's just something I remember reading about in one of my dictionaries. *The Dictionary of Useful Plants*, I think it's called. By—"

"Raahi!"

"Sorry. Guess that's irrelevant."

Sie's eyebrow arched. "But the name's suspicious. Who would name a business after some old herb like that?"

"The real question isn't who, but *where*," Raahi said.

Sie nodded. "No stairs. Right. Which means . . ." She began to walk slowly down the fourth-floor corridor again.

"Means what?" Raahi demanded as he followed her.

"We missed something." Sie ran a hand along the wall. It was painted a crisp light gray with bright white baseboard and crown molding. The wall was cool plaster under her fingers, rough and a bit chalky. Except in one place, where it felt warmer and smoother. She paused and rapped on the wall there. It sounded hollow.

"Something's hidden here," she said.

"Wormwood Properties?" Raahi asked.

There was a strange sound, like a speaker being switched on. *Crackle, fffbtzzzz.*

"Wormwood?" Raahi repeated more loudly.

"Welcome," a voice said over the speaker, sounding crackly. And then a whirring started. Somewhere in the wall, an electric motor had switched on.

A section of wall about four feet wide began to roll to the side. As the whirring of the motor grew louder, the section revealed a broad opening.

"I guess it's a password," Raahi said. "I had a hunch of sorts." He sounded rather pleased with himself.

"No, you didn't," Sie said. "That was just luck."

"Are we going in?" he asked.

Sie leading, they stepped through the entry and found themselves turning to the right and climbing another set of stairs. The panel slid closed behind them with more whirring and a snap that suggested it might have locked itself. "I'll blast it open on the way out," Sie said. "I don't like secrets."

Raahi smiled. It seemed to him that Sie's life was all about secrets.

The stairs lead to a narrow corridor with no windows, lit only by skylights of frosted glass in an angled ceiling. They walked so far that it seemed they must be at the end of the building, but the corridor, with a half step down, continued. Another two dozen steps forward, plus a half step up, and the corridor took a sharp turn to the left to reveal a single window at the far end. To the right of the window was a door. One door. It was made of varnished oak. There was no number. There was no buzzer.

Sie glanced out the window, which revealed that they seemed to have passed beyond the confines of Number 234 and apparently walked through the attic of the next building, so that they were now actually in the rear of the building that was directly next to Vose Gallery. "This must be it," Sie said. "Beside Mr. Vose's paintings."

Raahi nodded and raised his fist to knock on the door.

"Wait," Sie said. "There's something odd about it."

"Odd?"

"Not right. I don't like the feel of it. Someone's there."

"Not your aunt?"

Sie shrugged. "She might be, but our enemies might be there too." She was keeping her voice low, almost whispering.

"What do we do?" Raahi asked.

Sie thought. "Not be the first ones there when they answer our knock," she whispered. "Time for another illusion."

"Wolves? Those were really great!"

"Come back up the hall so we're out of sight around the corner."

Once there, she took him by the arm, held him still, and stared at him. Then she turned him around and continued to stare at him.

"Is there something wrong with my appearance?" Raahi asked. "Have I got something on me?"

"Shh. Let me work." Sie closed her eyes and began to chant. She wove complex, curving shapes in the air in front of her. She said something in some ancient language of power that was definitely not Latin, Greek, or Hindi.

Raahi rummaged through his memory, finally deciding that it might be an early Aramaic language associated with the Sasanian Empire. *But,* he reminded himself, *no one has spoken that language for a thousand years. In this world, at least,* he added, just as two bright columnar lights popped into view, floating beside them.

The bright columns blinked and shimmered and rotated as they began to darken and thicken into human forms. And there, standing right in front of them, were themselves! Raahi's double had a permanently puzzled frown while Sie's looked surprised, with raised eyebrows and slightly open mouth.

"They aren't perfect," she complained. "At school I made an illusion of myself that took three exams before it faded. I got an A+ in my illusions class. Too bad the illusion flunked my other exams, though." She turned and pointed, and the illusions set off down the hall toward the unmarked door ahead.

The real Sie and Raahi watched, peeking around the corner, as their doubles reached the door, raised their hands, and knocked in unison.

A motorized hum accompanied the swivel of a small camera mounted above the door. There was a long pause. The illusions were just raising their hands to knock again when the door swung inward. Large arms in dark suit-coats reached out and pulled the illusions inside. The door swung closed behind them with a snap.

Raahi and Sie, the real ones, ducked back around the corner. "It seems," Raahi said, "that we've found the hornet's nest."

"Do you think this is where they're headquartered?"

He shrugged. "One of their bases, anyway. I bet they're in other cities too. Did you know that there are 381 major metropolitan areas in the United States, although I thought the CIA was only supposed to operate on foreign soil according to its charter, which—"

"Raahi!"

"I'm just saying."

"Yes, but why would they want to hold Auntie captive?" Sie asked.

Raahi shrugged. "A person of interest? And she was captured when, ah, they knew more. Maybe they aren't so sure why they caught her now but they're still holding her."

"I asked the wrong question," Sie said, glancing up and down the corridor. "The real question is *where*."

"Here, of course." Raahi looked puzzled.

"Almost certainly here, but I mean *exactly* where." Sie crossed the hall and put her hand on the wall. "This is probably part of their rooms, yes?"

Raahi shrugged. "I think we may deduce, from the length of the hall and lack of any other doors, that their office suite is quite extensive."

"Does that mean yes?"

He nodded.

"Then let's take a look." She raised her hands again.

This time, Sie did not summon wind. That tended to be a noisy way to punch holes in things. Instead, she dug through her memory of alchemical equations and reactions and summoned enough acid to the wall that a section of it bubbled and hissed, then melted away, leaving steaming edges around an opening large enough for them to step through.

The arrival of their illusions at the front door must have attracted enough attention to empty out the rather boring looking office they stepped into. Gray metal desks occupied the main part of a beige-carpeted room, and on the far side, her arms taped to the arms of a chair, sat Great Aunt Generous. She looked quite pleased to see them.

"Guard the door, Raahi!" Sie called as she ran to the old woman and began to tear at the wide strips of sticky silver tape.

Raahi scanned the room, took note of the open door (which lead to another room of empty desks), and turned back. "How?"

"Weave a barrier or block their vision or something," Sie said, not really paying attention. The tape was very tough and hard to remove.

"Just dissolve the adhesive, dear," Aunt Gen said. "It will be quicker, and—ow—less painful."

"Good idea!" Sie held her hands over her aunt's arms and muttered. Curls of tape fell to the carpeted floor.

Aunt Gen rubbed her arms and, with Sie's help, got up. "Thank you! I knew you'd come through. Did you get my note?"

"In pieces. The finches must have run into trouble and asked some crows to help. But we can talk later," Sie said as she guided Aunt Gen through the hole in the wall.

Raahi was just stepping out after them when a commotion caught their attention. They turned to stare at the door to the room, the one from the adjoining office space. Raahi and Sie's illusions had just been pushed through. Several large men in dark suits followed, looking sternly annoyed.

"Clones?" the lead man asked his companions as they eyed the real Raahi and Sie (who, of course, looked remarkably like their illusions, right down to every detail of their clothing).

"Don't know, but it's trouble, and they've got the old lady," another man said. "Hey, you three! Stay right there!" Then he put a hand to his ear and whispered something.

Sie whispered, too, and the illusions faded discretely from sight.

"They'll be sending men to cut us off," Aunt Gen said. "They have telephones in their ears."

"Not anymore," Sie said. With a snap of her fingers, the men began to curse and hop on one leg with their heads tipped to the side and to hit their own ears and shake their heads madly. "I turned those ear things to hornets. Serves them right."

"Yes, I think it does," Aunt Gen said with a grin. "Shall we take advantage of the distraction, my dears?"

They hurried down the corridor, rushed around the corner, and stopped short. There were more men coming toward them, men with drawn guns and very angry looks on their faces. Leading them was Sie's mother.

CHAPTER 18

The Tide Turns

"You!" Sie's mother shouted. "What in the world do you think you're doing?"

"What are *you* doing!" Sie shouted back, her fists clenched. "Taping Auntie to a *chair!* Selling her *house!* Faking her ***death!*** I ought to, I ought to—"

"Hang on, Sie," Raahi said, taking her by the arm. "You actually oughtn't do anything, if you know what I mean."

"But she's *crazy*, she, she . . ." Sie subsided into silence, whether due to Raahi's grip, the men's guns (all of them pointing at her), or both.

"Did you really put my house up for sale?" Aunt Gen asked, addressing Sie's mother. When scowling silence seemed to confirm her question, she drew herself up and said, "Now, see here. As a government agent, you can't go around committing major crimes like fraud and robbery! This would be a very good time to make things right, and perhaps I just *might* be willing to forgive and forget, as they say. We shall have to see."

"Who, *me?*" Sie's mother sputtered into indignant response. "*You're* the one who, who . . ." But she paused, frowning, then turned to the nearest man. "Remind me what we're holding her on?" she demanded.

"Your orders, ma'am," he said. "But the specific charges were so highly classified that we haven't read them. We just picked her up for you. Don't you remember?"

"And taped her to a chair?" Sie demanded.

"She was permitted to lie down for eight hours each night so as to be fresh for questioning the next day," the man added, sounding defensive.

"And they *very* kindly offered me a carrot stick, a granola bar, and a cup of water each evening for dinner," Aunt Gen added. "*So* nice of them to help me with my diet. I've probably lost at *least* a dozen pounds in the past month, and Lord knows I wouldn't have had the discipline to starve *myself* like that!" A sweet if not entirely sincere grin followed this statement.

"You did all that to a *little old lady?*" Sie hissed, her hand beginning to weave something at her side.

Raahi took hold of her hand. "Ah, let's not do anything we might regret later," he said. "Anything else," he added with a glance at the large, rough-edged hole in the wall.

"You have not only attempted to break a high-value suspect out of custody, but you've also wantonly destroyed government property and, and . . . how *did* you make that hole, Silent?" her mother demanded.

"The most amazing coincidence," Aunt Gen hurried to say. "Really, I could hardly believe my eyes! The wall simply failed. Boom! And when the dust cleared, these nice young people happened to be coming down the hall. You really ought to have an engineer look at the entire building. It was terribly lucky that nothing fell on them as they walked by. Tut tut, I don't know *what* the government's coming to these days if this is how they run things." She shook her head sternly, a look of firm disapproval on her face.

"That's a ridiculously unlikely story," Sie's mother snapped. "In point of fact, we're investigating . . . what's our directive at this branch, Fredricks?" she demanded, turning to one of the men. "I can't seem to remember the exact details."

"Energized Variable Events and Non-Typical Stuff," he rattled off. "The EVENTS initiative, ma'am. We search for new weapons by studying things that violate the known rules of science. It was your ground-breaking memo on the subject that lead to our current research. Don't you recall?"

"I seem to be a bit vague on it. Perhaps the memo was classified at a higher level than even I have, and my memory of it had to be wiped. Now, where were we?"

"Apologizing for kidnapping Auntie, faking her death, and taking her house?" Sie's tone was sarcastic.

"Not to mention," Aunt Gen added, "discussing the impropriety of a very high-ranking, ah, 'government intelligence' agent, if that isn't an obvious oxymoron, abusing her position in order to seize control over an aging relative's estate." Aunt Gen paused for dramatic effect. "That's what this is all about, men, so you can put your guns away. Why, I wouldn't be surprised if *The Boston Globe* does a cover story on abuse of office, federal overreach of authority and so forth, with all of your photographs on the front page."

"We mustn't have that," one of the men said, frowning. "Central Investigation of Alchemy is supposed to be kept *entirely* invisible to the general public."

"Wait, I thought it was the Central Intelli—" Sie began, but Fredricks raised a hand to stop her. "That will do, miss. Our name isn't important. What *is* important is that no photographs are permitted. *Ever*. It would blow our cover."

"Indeed," Raahi agreed. "And so would a messy court case and the media circus surrounding it. This nice old woman is Officer Lee's—"

"*Senior Case Officer* Lee," Sie's mother corrected. "And who in the world are you?"

"I'm not important," Raahi said with a dismissive wave of the hand. "What's important is that this senior government agent has trumped up false charges against her own aunt and spirited her away to a safe house, I believe it is termed, in order to—"

"A Secure Area For Evaluation," another of the men corrected.

"Which, I imagine, is abbreviated as S-A-F-E," Raahi replied. "So, as I was saying, this officer of the law hid her own aunt in a safe house. Or office. Is there a bedroom, by the way, or did she have to sleep on the carpet? It doesn't look like a very comfort—"

"Raahi!" Sie interrupted.

"Yes, sorry. As I was saying," Raahi continued, "this government official faked her aunt's death and hid her in a secure government facility while taking control of her estate and putting her house up for sale. Not to mention making this girl homeless." He gestured rather dramatically toward Sie. "What," he continued, "do you do if there is a threat of a scandal such as, ah, this one?"

"That's classified. No, actually, I don't think it is," Fredricks said, frowning. "We CRIME, which stands for Close Ranks, Investigate, Minimize, and Eliminate."

"By 'eliminate,' you don't mean us?" Raahi hastened to ask.

"Only if we have to, and since you have no hard evidence, I don't think it will be necessary." He turned to Sie's mother. "But Officer Lee will have to restore your—"

"See here!" Sie's mother interrupted. "I'm *not* returning that house and all the valuables! I've already packed them up to go to the lab for further study!" Sie's mother looked outraged.

"What's to study?" Sie asked, gambling that her reweave would make the question a tough one.

"We're investigating . . . we need to find out how . . . well, I'll review the memo as soon as I get the proper clearance."

Fredricks exchanged looks with several other dark-suited men. They nodded.

"What we have here," Fredricks said, addressing Sie's mother, "is a Level Seven A-B-U-S-E-O-F-P-O-W-E-R."

"See here, Fredricks!" Sie's mother objected. "That's an outrageous accusation, and if you think I can't spell and don't know what you're talking about, you have another thing coming!"

"I wasn't spelling," he said. "It's an acronym. It stands for 'Abuse By Uncontrolled Senior Echelon Operative For Personal Or Wanton Enrichment and Reward.' And in such cases, we are required to secure the rogue agent, revoke her clearance, and M-O-P U-P, ma'am."

"I've never heard of these acronyms!" Sie's mother shouted. "What in the world does 'MOP UP' stand for?"

"I can't tell you," Fredricks replied, "now that your clearance has been revoked. Men?"

With a smooth turn, each man's gun was suddenly aimed at Sie's mother. "You'll be coming with us," another man said. "Jones, go get the roll of duct tape."

"I'm sorry for any inconvenience this may have caused," Fredricks said with a nod of his head in Aunt Gen's direction. "Ma'am. Girl. Boy. Good day." And then he turned and followed the group of stern, dark-suited men who were escorting Sie's mother away, despite her urgent protests.

With Raahi supporting Aunt Gen on one side and Sie on the other, they made their way to the elevator and Raahi pushed the button. "Hopefully you don't need a card to go down," he said.

"I would rather not ride that contraption," Aunt Gen said. "I think I'm strong enough to handle the stairs."

"I could weave a little supporting breeze," Sie offered.

"How nice. I don't suppose anyone would notice just this once, dear."

With a few gestures and a muttered chant, Silent brought a gentle but persistent wind into the hall (this time, Raahi noticed that Sie was speaking in Hindi).

"That's right, Silent, but not too much. I'll just sit back and . . ." Aunt Generous smiled. She was apparently leaning back on nothing. She began to float gently down the hall. When she reached the stairs, she turned and wafted softly downward, and they followed. There was a brief pause at the bottom of the first stairs as Sie melted the sliding panel away, then they hurried down the hall to the main stairs.

As they reached the lobby and headed for the oak front door, Sie happened to glance at the brass plate with its listing of various properties by floor. There was no longer a listing for Wormwood Suites—or anything at all—on the fifth floor. "What happened to the name?" she demanded.

"Lockdown mode?" Raahi guessed. "They've gone invisible."

"But how?" Sie demanded.

"The magic of technology," Raahi said with a shrug. "Maybe a multi-form metal that smooths over the lettering when an electrical charge is applied?"

"Let's not worry about them," Aunt Gen said. "And I don't think we need be unduly worried about your mother either. She's had ups and downs in her government career before."

"What will they do with her?" Sie asked.

"They'll relocate her, I should think, and there will be a demotion, but she'll be all right. Why, I wouldn't be surprised if we got another box of spices next Christmas, although I don't know what we'll do with it. The cupboard is already overstuffed with her smelly gifts as it is."

"Actually," Sie said, "she's thrown out all our food. And what's this about her being my adopt—"

"Dear me!" Aunt Gen interrupted. "Thrown it all away? Really!

Well, we shall just have to go shopping. Now that I've caught my breath, I do believe I'm feeling stronger than usual, my dear. A good night's sleep and I'll be better than new! I suspect the extreme diet has actually done me good." Then, with a warm smile toward both of them, she added, "Yes, I would greatly enjoy going on a shopping trip with you and your beau tomorrow, my dear."

"What? Wait one minute, Auntie! He's definitely not—look, I'm still fourteen and I *don't have* boyfriends!"

"Pardon me," Raahi said, "but Silent is correct. We are casual acquaintances. I would not even presume to claim to be friends. We met quite recently, unless you count sitting through an amazingly dull and misinformed science class together."

"You're at the local school, Raahi?" Aunt Gen asked.

"I was."

"Where those dreadful cousins go?" she continued.

"That's right, Auntie," Sie said. "I've been staying in their attic while you were a captive. I can't believe Mother did that to you!"

"To both of us, dear, but we will be more careful in the future. So, Raahi, do you live nearby?"

"Yes, ma'am. Near the cousins."

"Then it won't be such a long walk for you to come visit after Silent moves back in with me. As casual acquaintances, of course." She smiled.

"I could if Sie wanted me to," he said cautiously.

"You might as well," Sie said. "I'm getting used to you."

"Well, goodbye, then, and thank you for including me in your most interesting adventure." He gave a little half bow and turned to walk away.

Sie hurried to grab him by the arm. "Hold on," she said. "It might help if Auntie explained things to your mother so you don't get in trouble for missing dinner."

"Dear me, it *is* rather late," Aunt Gen agreed. "Young man, would you please flag down one of those automated yellow hacks? Oh, but you're modern, aren't you? I suppose you know them as taxi cabinets?"

"I'll get us a cab right away, Ms. Lee," Raahi said, smiling.

CHAPTER 19

Unpacking

The taxi dropped them outside of Raahi's door. There was a bad moment when they realized that none of them had any money to pay for it, but then Sie thought of the plastic card she'd used for groceries. Aunt Gen just shook her head and said, "Next time we go out, let's use the side door."

Raahi's mother came hurrying to their knock and made quite a fuss over him until he finally managed to calm her down and explain that he'd been helping a neighbor.

"With what?" she asked, and then they all took turns trying to explain what had happened without getting into *too* many suspicious details. In the end, she still looked puzzled, but was happy enough to have met Silent and Aunt Gen.

After the door had closed and they had walked back up the little path to the sidewalk, they stopped and Aunt Gen wrapped her arms around Sie and gave her a long hug. "I'm so proud of you," she said. "Now, we had best stop by the cousins' and explain that you'll be coming back to my house. And thank them for their hospitality, of course. And you probably have some belongings you need to collect?"

Sie rolled her eyes. "The cousins don't care what happens to me. They've gone away for vacation and rented out their house."

"My goodness! Where have you been staying, then?"

"I hadn't worked that out yet. You can get your house back from Mother—I mean legally, right?"

"I have excellent lawyers in both worlds, dear. Do you still have your key, by the way?"

Sie nodded. "I wouldn't give it to her. It's what she wanted, you know."

"Yes, I gathered. But since you rewove your story and she no longer remembers the key, I think we'll be perfectly safe. By the way, I was wondering . . ."

"What is it, Auntie?"

"Well, that boy seems quite the young gentleman and so very clever."

"Ye-es. I suppose he is."

"I have a dear old friend who runs the Boys' Academy of Alchemy and Magic. They recently moved to 374 Commonwealth Ave. It's a lovely new building with lots of space for labs."

"New in the side-door world, you mean. I know about it because some of my classmates at GALA have brothers at BAAM. From what I hear, it's a really good school."

"I shall speak to the headmaster and see that Raahi is enrolled right away."

"You can do that?" When Aunt Gen nodded, Sie smiled broadly and added, "Raahi will be very pleased, I think." Then she frowned. "But will his mother be willing to pay for it? She might not even have the right kind of money. Do they take money from the future, do you think?"

"He'll go on full scholarship, just like you. They need talented students. *Especially* from side worlds. There are so few people who can go back and forth, you see."

"You mean Raahi has, uh, talent?"

"Oh yes. He's quite magical. He just doesn't know it yet. They do such a poor job of educating talented young people in this world."

She shook her head disapprovingly. "Of course, he'll need to come by our house on the way to school each day."

"What, every morning? Why?" Sie looked quite startled.

"If he comes in our front door in time to go out the side door with you, it will all work out quite nicely," Aunt Gen said. "Otherwise, it might be difficult for him to get to school on time."

"Or at all," Sie agreed. "I see what you mean. So, do you think it's worth knocking on the cousins' door and asking the renters if I can get my things?"

"Of course," Aunt Gen said. "I'm sure they are reasonable people."

A few moments later, after knocking on the kitchen door and being loudly cursed and shouted at for interrupting them during dinner and being annoying neighbors and disturbing the peace and a great deal more, Aunt Gen frowned and said, "Perhaps they aren't reasonable, after all."

"It's just a change of clothes and a few books," Sie said. "I don't mind leaving them for now. But the birdcage . . ."

"Yes, we must have our birdcage back," Aunt Gen agreed. "I'm so glad you took it, though, my dear. Otherwise, I don't know how I would have reached you. Now, let's make sure this is a good time to retrieve our cage." She closed her eyes, hummed a fluting birdlike melody, and—her head disappeared from the neck up.

"Auntie! Are you all right?"

"Back again!" Auntie said cheerfully as her head reappeared. "I was just peeking around. That attic is not a proper bedroom at all, my dear. I can't believe they made you stay there. Tut tut! I shall have to have my solicitor arrange things so that your mother can't do something like this again. I should never have trusted her in the first place, but I needed someone plausible from the modern world, you see. However, given her recent behavior, it should be simple enough to convince a judge you're better off with me."

"Wait, you had her adopt me for legal purposes? Then who's my real mother?"

"Well, I suppose I should tell you all about it, but it's been a long day already. Would you be willing to wait until we get resettled?"

Sie frowned. "I don't like secrets."

"Yes, of course, and we'll clear things up over breakfast tomorrow. How's that?"

"I guess."

"And I'll instruct my lawyers to switch the paperwork so that I'm your legal guardian in both worlds. How's that?"

"You'll adopt me? That would be wonderful, Auntie!"

"It would be my pleasure, Sie. And then, should anything happen to me again, my house will go directly to you, along with the key."

"Nothing's going to happen to you, Auntie. Unless you keep doing risky things like sticking your head up through the bottom of birdcages," Sie pointed out. "Is my real mother from the side door world?"

Aunt Gen held up a hand to stop her. "Tomorrow, I promise. Now, do you suppose, my dear, that a wind might come up?"

"Wind?" Sie repeated, puzzled. It was a lovely, calm summer evening.

"Just enough to break the attic window. And then, perhaps, to float the birdcage down to us? If you'll take care of that, I'll go hail an automated hack with enough room for the birdcage *and* us. I *do* so dislike those modern yellow ones where you have to stuff yourself into a cramped little seat." She turned and stepped to the curb, her hand raised.

Sie eyed the attic window. With a muttered chant, it burst in, and so did several others on the floor below. "I hope their bedrooms fill up with flies and mosquitos!" she muttered as she raised her hands and gestured to guide the birdcage out the window. It levitated there, rotating slowly next to the house, until Sie waved for it to come down. In a moment, it had landed gracefully next to Aunt Gen and the very antique, shiny black taxi she had summoned.

The taxi had open-spoke wheels and a varnished oak carriage in back, with two rows of seating and a high roof.

"It's a Model T depot hack, my dear. Loads of room. I don't know why they ever took them off the road."

The driver tipped his old-fashioned cap and said, "Home, ma'am?" as if he already knew just where they were going. Then, with a *flu-bitty-flubbity-pop!* and a grinding of gears, they were off.

And although there was quite a bit of unpacking to do and Silent's bed frame had to be put back together, it took them remarkably little time. "We shall bend a rule or two, I think," Aunt Gen said once she saw the state of the house. "Exigent circumstances, my dear. Exigent circumstances." And then they both went through the rooms, muttering and gesturing toward overstuffed boxes, so that all their beloved belongings flew back into place without a single accident. The plywood sheet nailed over the side door was popped away by sending it with a relocation chant to the middle of the office where Aunt Gen had been held captive. "Just to remind them not to bother us again," Aunt Gen said with a twinkle in her eyes. "And to give them one more inexplicable event to think about, since I assume the building has been securely locked up for the night."

Soon the house had been returned to the familiar home that Silent had always known and loved and finches were chirping sleepily in the birdcage again.

They sat in the parlor together, sipping hot cocoa and talking. Aunt Gen poured it out of a chipped old earthenware pitcher since Sie's mother had taken the silver ones, but they didn't care; they were just happy to be back together and home again. And then the old clock on the mantle struck eleven and they headed for bed. But before she went upstairs, Sie paused to pull a piece of cloth over the cage. As she did, she leaned over and whispered, "Would you be so kind as to ask an owl to bring Raahi this note? It can tap on his window. I'm sure he'll come to see what it is." The note she handed in through the cage read, "Thanks for all your help today! Guess what? We have surprise news that I think you'll like. Come by at teatime tomorrow and Auntie will tell you about it."

"Are you letting Raahi know?" Aunt Gen asked from the stairs.

"I invited him to tea. I thought you could tell him then."

"Excellent! Perhaps I'll bake some scones. Oh, and in the morning," Aunt Gen said, "we shall call on good old Mr. Vose to thank him for helping you and to see if we can't cure him of *his* key-weariness. I think your so-called mother, may she rest peacefully while duct-taped to her cot, accidentally showed me how to rediscover one's magic."

"Auntie!" Sie cried, an excited grin spreading across her face. "Are you all better? I noticed you did more workings than usual tonight, what with all the unpacking and everything."

"Yes, my dear. I feel ten years younger. Who would have guessed? All it took was a month of the strictest diet, combined with the rigors of daily cross-examination. I declare, my dear, I'm as fit as a fiddle. And not some dusty old Stradivarius, either. A nice, new one from one of those music shops on Newbury Street."

"I don't think they sell violins on Newbury Street, Auntie. It's shakes and high heels and spa treatments now."

"Not on *my* Newbury Street, Sie. Now come to bed, please, and tomorrow morning we'll go out the side door and have a lovely day in the city."

CHAPTER 20

Owl Time

Sie felt a strange and pleasant sense of contentment as she climbed into her bed that night. However, just as she was about to fall asleep, she sat up abruptly. "Darn!" she exclaimed. "I left the envelope with my birth certificate in the cousins' attic. And now that the attic window's broken, someone's bound to go up there tomorrow to fix it."

"You're right," came Aunt Gen's voice. She had just come to the door. "The same thought occurred to me as I was getting into bed. I'd hidden some rather important papers with that bird cage, hadn't I?"

"I'm sorry," Sie said.

"Don't worry, Dear. We'll just have to send an owl through the window to hunt for them. Come on."

And that is how Silent Lee found herself going out the front door again with her aunt, by moonlight in their nightgowns and bathrobes, with the depot hack and its whiskered old driver waiting at the curb. *How did she summon him?* Sie wondered as they climbed in, *and how did he get here?* The man and his vehicle were obviously from the side door world, and yet here he was again, as if boundaries meant nothing to him. But Aunt Gen was not in a talking mood, so Sie had to content herself with her own thoughts as the vehicle sputtered and grumbled through the oddly quiet nighttime streets of modern Boston.

THE END

Author's Note

The places in the book are real. You can visit the addresses and walk all the routes mentioned, but I don't know if you'll bump into Silent and Raahi. If you do, I'm sure you'll recognize them. Be sure to say hi.

As for Silent's school, GALA, I know the building well, and it is indeed a magical old edifice. It was the house my dad grew up in and my great-grandmother used to invite us there for holidays. When I went back recently, a caretaker really did say it was being remodeled for a princess as he shooed us off. Maybe he just wanted to send us away with an interesting story. Or else it was the truth. You can't always tell, can you?

I also am acquainted with the building housing the Boys' Academy of Alchemy and Magic, but only in this world, where it provides a home for the Harvard Club of Boston. I stayed there for the night and had the strangest dreams about boys doing magical pranks on each other when their instructors weren't looking, so I'm pretty darn sure it is indeed a school of magic in the side world.

I drew on places around Back Bay that have meaning to me, but many other people have walked the same streets and I hope they don't take offense at my including names and places that may be relevant to them too. I don't, for instance, know the Vose family personally, but my great grandparents decorated their house with the gallery's paintings and I still have a few looking over me now, so I can attest to the fact that there is magic to be found there.

If you're anywhere near Boston, you ought to visit the Newbury Street art galleries (there are still some wonderful ones to be found). Also the Boston Public Library's main building and the other grand old buildings in the neighborhood. If it's warm, go for a ride on the Swan Boats in the Common, like Raahi and Sie will in a future book—but try not to fall in, even if Raahi does. As for the Shake Shack, last I knew, it was still there. After all that art and architecture, you might want to pop in for some refreshment. But do keep an eye out for strange men in black suits, especially if they seem to be keeping an eye on *you*.

About Alex Hiam

Hmm, what to say? The story really is the thing, but I can tell you that I've written and illustrated more than thirty books, also that I'm old enough to have gone to school at the tail end of the era in which some boys and girls were still educated separately at strict boarding schools. I was expected to study Latin and Greek, just like Sie, although they seemed to have left out the magical uses of these ancient languages, leaving it to me to discover them later on. (The Tozzer Library of Anthropology at Harvard has some remarkable old manuscripts . . .)

I have five children, all of whom love to read, which could explain my focus on magical stories, or at least it offers a ready excuse. My daughter Sadie was the first to read and edit this book, and as always, proved a great help. Also, like Silent, I'm adopted, but from where, I can't say for sure. My research hints at a deeper mystery that seems to be beyond the reach of detection so far, at least in *this* world...

The first Silent Lee adventure began as a series of eagerly scribbled notes on a visit to Back Bay with my brother and sister-in-law and my wife and daughters to see a cousin perform in the Cirque du Soleil. Tickets were limited and only "the girls" went to the performance, so my brother and I spent the day walking the neighborhoods to scope out locations for this book.

My father's grandmother, Jane Webster, was the only grandparent I knew as a child, but on my mother's side we have a number of quite interesting ancestors who inspired my art and writing when I was young, including illustrator Tasha Tudor and author-naturalist Thornton Burgess, whose work I grew up on. Also, of interest to me as an author, designer William Starling Burgess drew up the first version of Times New Roman, which is now the most widespread font. The font, or some modern variation on it, is used in most of the books I've published so far. It's fun for me to see my ancestor's hand in my books.

Speaking of books, I personally admit to favoring independent bookstores over chains and online emporiums. Local stores have owners and staff who work diligently to nurture the magic of books. In fact, a local bookstore is often a magical land unto itself, except that, unlike most magical lands, which are quite hard to find, the portal leading to it is conveniently unlocked during business hours. If you're exploring Silent's neighborhood, be sure to stop by Trident Booksellers & Cafe, Newbury Comics, and Bromer Booksellers, just to mention a few.

But enough about me. I bet you're wondering what's next for Silent Lee! I'm very interested in her story and am working on adventures two and three right now. I can report that she and Raahi will get caught up in a world-wide conspiracy that takes them through another doorway, this one in the back of a hotel closet. They emerge in the side-door world, but not anywhere near Boston. In Oxford, actually. Across the ocean. Where the Custodians are trained. But their magical college is in serious trouble, and so is the planet unless Si and Raahi can get things under control. (A sample chapter is appended.)

As for the midnight expedition, yes, Si and Aunt Gen eventually do retrieve her birth certificate—after an unexpected encounter with the Custodian from the Boston Public Library who says something in secret to Aunt Gen.

Sie gets just a glimpse of the puzzling document before Aunt Gen hides it away again. Why is her birth certificate puzzling? Because it *does not list her mother's name*, nor anyone she's ever heard of. It lists her mother as a Ms. LeGreen. Sue O. LeGreen to be specific. Also puzzling: her birth date, while accurate as to month and day, has the year badly wrong. A typo, Aunt Gen says dismissively. But what a typo! If it were true, Sie would be over one hundred years old. *This won't be any use in the modern world,* Sie thinks, annoyed. *But at least they don't question your right to an education at GALA.*

Silent Lee and The Oxford Adventure

Alchemy, Level Six

Alchemy class was held in a long, narrow, marble-floored room with high windows on one side, a run of blackboard down the other, and a tin-covered workbench, also quite long, with tall stools. The instructor stood near the door. The students joked that she wanted to be the first to leave if an experiment went wrong (but it may have been true).

Silent Lee had taken alchemy since first grade, and now she was in the top-level class with a dozen other advanced students, most of them seniors and several years older than her. Unfortunately her best friend, Ali, was not with her. Things tended to explode when Ali did lab work, so she was still at a much lower level.

In the first lab session of that fall, Sie found herself sitting between "The Twins": Ruby on her left, long blond hair swishing over the burners as she leaned in front of Sie to talk to her sister, Lula. Similarly, Lula's long blonde hair seemed to want to ignite itself whenever she leaned over to whisper to Ruby. (They were seniors, just starting their twelfth year.)

The twins whispered and giggled and ignored the instructor, but, annoyingly, they were naturals. Alchemical experiments fell in place for them, even when Sie was certain they had used the wrong proportions. "It's all very well if *you* don't want to listen," she muttered, pushing blonde hair away from her gas burner and the beaker and retort perched above it, "but I can't hear when you're talking!"

"Miss Lee. Did you have something you wished to contribute?" It was Master Medera, a stern, thin, tight-lipped woman with white hair pulled back in a very firm bun. She wore simple black full-length dresses and, when teaching, a black canvas apron.

"I'm sorry," Sie said. "I didn't mean for you to hear me." And of course, as soon as she said this, she regretted it.

The master put down her chalk and walked along the workbench until she was standing right behind Sie. "What, precisely, is it that you don't want me to hear?" she hissed.

"I, I didn't mean it that way," Sie hurried to explain, trying to look over her shoulder but unable to turn quite far enough to see Miss Medera clearly. "I was just . . ." And then she realized that she ought not tattle on the twins, because that was considered poor form and if she did, they would probably find a way to sabotage her lab work.

"Were you asking the twins for help?" Miss Medera leaned over the bench and her eyes swept along it, taking in Sie's careful progress (she had been following each step and taking time to measure accurately), compared to the startling progress of the twins. "Isn't this remarkable?" Miss Medera added, sounding quite pleased. "Ruby and Lula have already completed today's lab! Very nice work, girls, but don't help Silent. She ought to do it for herself. Now," she added, as she walked back to the front of the room, "who can tell me what this sequence is intended to produce?"

Silent's hand went up right away. Based on the drawings on the board, she could see that the product of their experiment was supposed to be a sweet elixir that contained a small amount of *Sa'āda*, or human happiness, according to *Kimiya-yi Sa'ādat*, an ancient alchemical text.

Miss Medera frowned at Sie and waited for another hand to go up. Finally Hilda, another twelfth grader, provided the answer.

"Very good. Now get back to work, and no more talking! I want you to have your results by end of class. We'll test them on each other before we leave."

On each other? Sie thought, glancing at the twins, who were whispering again and seemed very amused. *I hope I don't have to try theirs!*

Sie finished her work a few minutes before the bell and looked up as the instructor cleared her throat. "Turn off your burners and speak a cooling charm, please. Now, each of you turn to your neighbor and offer them a teaspoon of your elixir. Just one spoonful. If you've done it correctly, that should be enough to keep you in a good mood for the rest of the day."

By the time Silent had put away her lab equipment and packed up her notes, she was crying. Tears just insisted in raining down her cheeks and onto her blouse, and she could barely stifle sobs as she hurried to meet her friend Ali in the lounge. She had already soaked her handkerchief (all the girls carried them at that school; disposable tissues hadn't been invented yet in that world).

"Sie! What's the matter?" Ali looked alarmed. "Did something bad happen?"

Silent, who under normal circumstances never cried, had to wipe her face on her sleeve. "No, *sob*, it was The Twins, they did something to their, *sob*, elixir to give it an opposite effect."

"It was supposed to make you happy?"

Sie nodded and sniffed.

"We should report them!"

"On the first day?" Sie asked, wiping with the other sleeve. "I don't want to start out on the wrong foot. It's going to be a, *sniff*, terrible year! *Sniff. Sniff.* Do you think you can take this off me?"

"An alchemical reaction? No spell can counter that. Did you complete *your* elixir?"

Sie nodded, bleary eyed, and sat down with a thump at one of the many round tables in the student lounge.

"Get up. Quick!" Ali tugged her to her feet. "Before the next lab starts!" And then she was hurrying Silent out of the lounge, down the stairs to the basement, and, with a brief stop to hide in a broom closet while several masters walked past, into the lab itself.

The door was ajar, and no one was there. "Okay, where's yours? You always do them right."

Sie began to sob quietly into her soaking wet handkerchief. "There's no use! *Sniff, sniff.* "I'll never pass this class! What will Auntie think of me when I flunk out?"

"Get a hold of yourself," Ali hissed. "Someone's going to hear us." She hurried to the far end of the lab and tried to turn the brass handles to open the big cabinets. "Locked," she announced. "Come here. I'm not as good as you at openings."

Sie did not respond.

"Oh well, here goes," Ali said. "*Vi aperta armarium!*" she added in a louder voice, her hands held up, palms toward the cupboard.

Sie stopped blowing her nose and turned to see. At first, nothing happened. Then there was the sound of glass breaking. Ali frowned and tried the handles. "Still locked," she complained. "Maybe you should try."

Then there were more cracks and snaps and shattering sounds, louder and louder, as if everything inside the cupboard was breaking all at once. "Darn it!" Ali exclaimed, backing up. "That's not supposed to—"

"Mane! Morari! Restitutuere integritatem, statim!" It was Sie, rushing toward Ali and the cabinet, and shouting spells as fast as she could.

The sounds stopped.

They looked at each other.

Sie reached out and, with a muttered *obex laxo*, tried the handles.

The doors swung slowly open.

The shelves were all in neat order, jars and beakers and retorts and urns and the little drawers with their little labels for ingredients, just as they ought to be. And there, in the middle of one shelf, was a small vial labeled, Silent Lee, Experiment #1. Ali reached for it, but Silent said, "Let me." Tears were still streaming down her cheeks, but she seemed much calmer. Perhaps the urgency of the situation had taken precedence over the induced sadness of her mood.

"Drink some. Drink it all," Ali hissed. "And hurry! I hear foot-steps in the hall!"

And that was just the first day of school. Sie hoped they might already have put the worst of the semester behind them. She could not possibly have imagined all the other things that were about to go wildly and dangerously wrong.

CPSIA information can be obtained
at www.ICGtesting.com
Printed in the USA
LVHW011135170820
663373LV00003B/237

9 781635 580112